Pills to Purpose

A True Story of a Pharmacist

Ritesh Shah, RPh

TABLE OF CONTENTS

Author's Note

If you are holding this book in your hands, I want to begin by saying thank you for your love and support. Your belief in our mission fuels the passion that drives our work forward.

This is not just a collection of memories or a timeline of events. It is a piece of my heart — and my family's heart — offered to you with sincerity and love.

Pills to Purpose was born out of deep pain, but also deep hope. It is a story of loss, resilience, and the realization that true healing begins when we stop asking, "Why me?" and start asking, "How can I serve?"

As a pharmacist for over two decades — and as a husband married to another compassionate pharmacist — I have witnessed both the beauty and the brokenness of our healthcare system. I have seen patients forced to choose between medicine and food, between treatment and survival.

This book reflects on the lessons I've learned at the pharmacy counter, in the community, at hospitals, health fairs, and even from the back of my car during the pandemic — anywhere and everywhere there was a need. It chronicles a journey sparked by a simple yet profound realization: healthcare must go beyond pills and prescriptions. It must reach into the realm of empathy.

This is the story of an everyday pharmacist who chose to go beyond the call of duty. It is about seeing the person behind the prescription, and understanding that treatment must be not only physical, but emotional and spiritual as well.

It is a testimony to how loss can ignite purpose — and how a life dedicated to service can transform grief into something breathtakingly meaningful.

The stories in this book are not just mine. They belong to every patient, every volunteer, every supporter who walked this path with us.

Together, we've proven that ordinary people can create extraordinary change when compassion leads the way.

Whether you are a healthcare professional, a caregiver, a patient, or someone searching for hope, I pray you find a piece of yourself in these pages. May it remind you that even the smallest acts of kindness can light up the darkest nights.

Thank you for allowing me to share this journey with you.

With gratitude and service,

Ritesh Shah

Ritesh Shah, RPh
Community Pharmacist

Dedication

To my baby sister, Rena (aka Munni). Your vibrant spirit, unwavering kindness, and infectious laughter continue to illuminate my path. Your simplicity and your love for me and the family were never understood properly, and as I was getting closer to you from far away in New Jersey, God had a different plan. This book, and the work it represents, is a testament to your beautiful life and a dedication to the legacy of compassion you left behind. May it serve as a gentle reminder that your presence in this world was a gift, and your lessons of love, humility, and selflessness will live on forever.

To my family, Asha, Sarthak, and Krina, for their unwavering love and support throughout my journey, especially during times of profound loss and profound challenge. Asha, the better pharmacist, your strength and resilience have been my constant inspiration. Your ability to see the silver lining in every cloud has taught me valuable lessons in perseverance and optimism. Sarthak, my doctor son, who understands me more and never verbalizes his emotions, but always supports me silently, showing his love in countless ways. And my beautiful princess, Krina, thank you for encouraging me to finish writing this. Your feedback and support have helped shape every word, and I am eternally grateful for your belief in me. You are truly a light in our family. This book, and the sacrifice it represents, is a pledge of my love and gratitude to each of you. We are all appreciative of your positive energy and guidance. In the same spirit, this book is dedicated to all the mentors and friends who have been by my side.

To the countless patients whose stories are woven into these pages—your struggles, your resilience, and your unwavering hope have shaped my purpose and fueled my commitment to serving others. Each encounter with you has been a lesson in compassion and strength, reinforcing my belief in the power of human connection. God allowing me to serve so many patients in need over my 20 years working in the community makes me feel complete as a pharmacist. The bonds I've formed and the moments of healing witnessed have marked these years with meaning beyond measure. I've often felt your pain from behind the counter, steering my soul and heart toward giving and helping. Every prescription I filled held stories of courage and tears of relief, reminding me of the profound impact we can have on each other's lives.

This book is a tribute to your strength and a recognition of your invaluable contributions to my life's work. As I continue my journey, may this book serve as a testament to the enduring spirit of service that defines us all—a testament to the power of giving. And finally, to all those who believe in the power of community and the transformative potential of compassionate care, may this story inspire you to find your own purpose and to make a difference in the world, one act of kindness at a time. I hope that it encourages you to embrace the healing power of service and the profound joy that comes with helping others. May we all strive to leave a legacy of love and service as meaningful as Rena's. May your journey through these pages reignite your passion for service and remind us all that even the smallest acts of kindness can ripple through someone's life.

You know what he did. He actually acted upon it just to make the world a better and safer place.

I am not sure how to say it about him because it's me. How do I see him as an I? Why did he do what he did and is still doing it? This is where he found the peace and purpose he had been searching for. His journey began with small, seemingly insignificant gestures that grew into a lifelong commitment to service as a pharmacist. Even though I have been a pharmacist for almost 30 years, it took me 15 years to discover my passion for serving and helping others — 15 years to become a true pharmacist. It was only then that the real journey began.

That journey started when I discovered the power of medicine to heal, and I found my purpose in helping others through their health struggles. The journey started when I discovered the power of medicine to heal, and I found my purpose in helping others through their health struggles. It was a calling that resonated with every fiber of my being. I threw myself into my studies, determined to learn everything I could about how to help with pharmacy and its impact on health for those who had no means of getting these services. I immersed myself in the world of pharmacy and medicine, dedicating countless hours to understanding the complexities of the human body and the potential of pharmaceutical interventions. I was driven by an inner calling to make a difference and provide care for those in need. My dedication to helping others through this noble profession came by paying a big price.

Let me step back as I juggled long hours of studying and working at the pharmacy, often sacrificing sleep and personal time to hone my skills and knowledge. I pushed myself to the limit, fueled by the deep desire to make a positive impact.

One evening, as I labored over a particularly challenging time in my personal life, I received a call that changed everything. The challenge of helping others, especially those who don't have anything. On the other end of the line was a community health organization offering me the opportunity to volunteer my pharmaceutical expertise in underserved areas. Filled with a mix of excitement and trepidation, I accepted the challenge within me without hesitation.

It was a big decision to make, but I was going to do it because of the unwavering support of my wife, an extremely talented and dedicated woman. She stood by me and shared my passion for serving others. She encouraged me to listen to my heart and follow my dreams, reminding me that true fulfillment comes from using our gifts to benefit others. That decision led to a life-changing journey, one that took me to various communities in Monmouth County where access to healthcare and medicines was scarce. I found myself working long hours, sometimes in challenging conditions, as I balanced the tremendous responsibilities of running a successful GPO and a pharmaceutical warehouse along with a medical cannabis dispensary. But seeing the impact, which was often immediate, made it worth it. I realized that all the hard work and sacrifices were worth it when I saw the genuine smiles and gratitude of the people I was able to help. Their heartfelt thanks and the visible relief on their faces became my greatest motivation, driving me to continually search for ways to improve access to essential medications via pharmacy needs and healthcare. The sense of purpose that propelled me forward in my journey only grew stronger with each life I touched, and I knew that I was exactly where I was meant to be - making a real difference in people's lives through my work as a pharmacist.

Acknowledgments

Mom and Dad, for everything you have done for me. Lord Krishna and my teachers for installing values and teaching me. To my amazing, talented, and beautiful wife Asha, I am totally incomplete without her, and my wonderful kids Sarthak and Krina, aka my family. Especially both my brothers, Chetan Bhai and Jignesh, and my friends in India, Dhaval and Vairanya, whom I can't thank enough for their love and friendship. And here in the United States, I can't forget the powerful Ten Stars group and my Pinchu Kapoor WhatsApp group. Senator Vin Gopal came into my life as a friend almost 20 years ago, and I have learned so much from him during this amazing journey, especially about unconditional friendship. Senator Raj Mukherji, whom I met through Vin, has been a guiding torch. Dr. Tushar Patel helped instill Seva in me through the medical camps. Dr. Naveen Mehrotra is a treasure I will cherish for life. Joe Howe, Chief O'Hare, Dr. Rakesh Parikh, Elizabeth (COVID Testing site – Ed Oatman), Indian Health Camp of NJ (IHCNJ), SKN Foundation, and Jay Bhai Dhaduk, who has always held my hand when I was lost in troubling situations and guided me to make better decisions. Pritiben, my sister—through her, I now see Rena. Ayan Davis, my Program Director at Ritesh Shah Charitable Pharmacy, all the volunteers, and the board members.

Early Childhood, Education, and Pharmacy School

I was born and raised in an upper-middle-class household, surrounded by a large, multi-family setting where everyone lived together. In such an environment, I learned early on the importance of compassion, hard work, and the value of education and unity. Growing up in a tight-knit family, I cherished the moments we spent together, learning from the wisdom of my elders and building bonds that shaped my sense of belonging.

I spent my days playing cricket, forming teams, and organizing weekend games with neighborhood kids, some of whom came from just above the poverty line. Creating a strong sense of community and teamwork, those childhood experiences laid the foundation for my future endeavors. I remember how some of my friends couldn't afford to chip in for a cricket ball. I'd cover their part when I could, not just because they were good players, but because they mattered to me. That sense of responsibility taught me early on how to build trust: give something, earn their trust, and people will follow your lead. Through those games, I was unknowingly learning about leadership; how to bring people together, how to look out for others, and how to make space for fun while making sure everyone felt included.

Today, working as a pharmacist in the U.S., those values are still with me. I carry the same sense of responsibility and empathy into my work, making sure each patient feels heard and cared for. In my role, I work tirelessly to advocate for the wellness of those who entrust me with their health, drawing upon the lessons of camaraderie. I aim to foster a comforting and inclusive environment for all my patients, building on the foundation of trust and understanding that I learned in my formative years. I prioritize open communication and patient education, empowering individuals to take an active role in their own well-being. In doing so, I hope to make a positive impact on the lives of those in my community, just as I did for my teammates on the field.

Preface

Some journeys are chosen. Others are written through loss, love, and the quiet realization that everything we live through prepares us for something greater.

I never set out to create a charitable pharmacy. My journey began with a simple desire — to help people in meaningful ways as a pharmacist. Whether it meant flavoring a child's medication, delivering life-saving prescriptions through brutal winters, or staying open late for a patient in crisis, I believed pharmacy was never just about pills. It was about people. It was about purpose.

In 2003, I opened Bayshore Homecare Pharmacy in Holmdel, New Jersey. One small space became many — each new location an opportunity to serve more patients, touch more lives, and stand in the gap when the healthcare system fell short. My wife, Asha, stood beside me every step of the way. Together, we faced heartbreaking disparities: seniors rationing insulin, families choosing between medicine and meals. We did what we could because that's what we were called to do.

Then came the pandemic. COVID-19 exposed cracks that had always been there. From our garage, cars, and community centers, we fought to protect those most at risk — delivering supplies, administering vaccines, and holding hands when fear felt overwhelming. But nothing prepared me for the loss that followed.

In October 2021, my beloved sister Rena passed away during what was meant to be a joyful Diwali reunion. Her loss broke something inside me, and in that heartbreak, something else was born.

Rena had always encouraged me to help those who had nothing. Her spirit, her strength, her belief in kindness became the seed of a greater mission. In her memory, we founded the Ritesh Shah Charitable Pharmacy, the first of its kind in New Jersey. A place where no one would be turned away for lack of money. A space where compassion and dignity are dispensed alongside medicine.

This book is the story of that transformation from grief to purpose, from personal sorrow to a public promise. It is both a memoir and a mission, a reflection on what it means to serve and to heal, not just others, but yourself.

If you've ever faced loss, walked through pain, or searched for deeper meaning, I hope these pages remind you: your story isn't over. Sometimes, our greatest purpose is born from our deepest wounds.

Let this journey be proof that even in the face of unimaginable loss, light can shine again, brighter than ever.

Introduction

My journey from a small town in India, Talod, to founding New Jersey's first charitable pharmacy has been anything but straightforward. It's been a path marked by difficult choices, deep lessons, and moments I never could have predicted. The transition from the quiet solitude of my childhood to the fast-paced intensity of pharmacy school was jarring, but the academic rigor was only the beginning. Coming from a non-English background, entering an English-speaking college brought its own challenges. Between the demanding coursework and the pressure, not just to succeed but sometimes just to pass, I often found myself overwhelmed. Still, in the middle of that chaos, I found camaraderie and support in my fellow classmates. I lived in the dorms at ARCP in V.V. Nagar, a religious institution where I met Rashesh, Bidhen, and Pravin, who later became monks in the BAPS organization. Around that same time, Rakshit Raval, now known as Gnanvatsal Swami, offered occasional coaching and advice that stayed with me. I was amazed. I kept asking myself, how can someone give up everything to serve others like that? Their commitment left me both inspired and searching. The friendships formed during those late nights of studying proved invaluable, offering not just intellectual support but also the emotional sustenance needed to persevere. Those four years at APC taught me more than pharmacy. They shaped my values. I learned about service, faith, and the quiet strength of helping someone in need, while still finding joy in each day. I am also very thankful to all the Sants who mentored me and helped me grow as a leader. During my time there, I served as president of our study circle and built a community of around 500 members, including students beyond the pharmacy college. Through that experience, I also saw something that stuck with me. Some of my friends came from poor families. I noticed them skipping meals, sometimes lunch, sometimes dinner, and I couldn't ignore it. I didn't come from a wealthy background either, but I helped however I could. They were my friends, and I saw their struggles up close.

Later, those same challenges showed up in my professional life. Working in a busy retail pharmacy in a low-income neighborhood exposed me to the stark realities of healthcare disparities. I witnessed firsthand the struggles of patients facing financial barriers to accessing life-saving medications. My first job was at Katz Pharmacy in Brooklyn as a pharmacy Technician. That was quite an experience where we were dealing with patients with Medicaid and some of those who had just enough money to buy one- or two-weeks' supply. The desperation in their eyes, the agonizing choices they were forced to make, and their resilience in the face of adversity deeply affected me. These experiences were pivotal in shaping my vision to become a pharmacy owner and establish an organization that would remove financial barriers to medication access and provide holistic care to vulnerable populations. But that was a mistake and a dream only. It was in those early encounters, those moments of intense human connection, that the seeds of my future work were sown.

This book delves into the personal and professional aspects of that journey, weaving together stories from the pharmacy and intimate reflections on my personal path, particularly the profound loss of my sister and how that loss ultimately propelled me towards creating a legacy of compassion and service. This is a narrative of resilience. It's about finding clarity in chaos, and about how, sometimes, the hardest experiences make us who we are. It is my hope that this book will inspire readers to embrace their own passions, to find meaning in service to others, and to strive to make a positive impact on their communities. The path wasn't always easy; there were countless hurdles, times when the vision seemed too distant to grasp, and moments of doubt that threatened to dismantle it all. Yet, with each challenge faced and overcome, the purpose became clearer, the mission more urgent.

Chapter 1: The Calling of a Pharmacist

The transition from the familiar comfort of my home to life at V.V. Nagar, where pharmacy school awaited, was a turning point. The quiet solitude of the woods and open land was replaced by the constant hum of city life, a symphony of sirens, big paved roads of Bhai Kaka Marg, and the hurried footsteps of countless strangers. It was both thrilling and daunting, a new chapter in my life filled with unknowns.

Pharmacy school brought a whole new kind of pressure. Gone were the days of leisurely afternoons spent exploring the woods; now, every waking moment seemed consumed by textbooks, lectures, and endless hours spent studying. Organic chemistry, pharmacology, and pharmaceutics became my new realities, demanding a level of focus and discipline I had never experienced before. Despite how intense the coursework was, I found real comfort in the friendships I built with my classmates. It was a tough curriculum; a constant struggle between trying to understand complicated chemical formulas and learning how to actually prepare and give out medications. But even with all that pressure, we still found time to laugh, share stories, and push through together. Those moments of connection, even in the middle of all the stress, kept us going.

The pressure was intense. Exams felt like they were always around the corner, hanging over us and making every day feel heavier than the last. Coming from a Gujarati-medium background, I struggled at first to follow the English lectures, especially when it came to understanding equations and theories. But I held on to determination like it was the only thing I had. There was so much to absorb—drug names, chemical interactions, clinical cases—it felt like I was drowning in information some days.

The competition didn't help either. It wasn't openly aggressive, but it was always there, quietly pushing everyone to keep up. Most of my classmates were incredibly focused and talented, all trying to do their best in one of the most demanding fields. Sleep became a luxury, a rare commodity I often sacrificed at the altar of academic achievement. Weekends were devoted to studying, often blurring into a continuous cycle of lectures, labs, and late-night study sessions fueled by copious amounts of coffee. I was lucky, though, to meet Dr. Sailesh Sir and his family. Dr. Sailesh's calm nature and wise advice helped guide me during some of the hardest stretches.

Even though it was all-consuming, we still found time to help each other through. There was a bond that formed among us, people working toward the same goal, facing the same uphill climb. We supported each other through late-night study sessions, shared notes, and offered encouragement when morale dipped. We formed study groups, collaborating on complex problems and quizzing each other to strengthen our understanding of the material. These friendships, forged in the fires of academic pressure, proved invaluable, providing not only intellectual support but also emotional sustenance.

It wasn't just the academic load that presented challenges; there were also the personal sacrifices that inevitably accompanied the pursuit of a demanding professional education. Maintaining relationships with friends and family back home became increasingly difficult. Phone calls were shorter, visits were rare, and replying to emails took longer than I liked. That distance started to feel heavier over time. I missed the simple things like talking with family, eating home-cooked food, and just being around people who knew me. Balancing school with taking care of my own mental and physical health turned into its own kind of struggle. One of the few things that helped me stay grounded was exercising regularly. It gave me a break from everything and helped me let go of the stress I was carrying around.

When I started working after pharmacy school, a lot of those challenges followed me. My first job was at a busy retail pharmacy in a low-income neighborhood. It was there that I really began to see how broken the healthcare system could be. I saw patients struggling to afford their medications, making agonizing choices between food and essential prescriptions. I witnessed the frustration of insurance denials, the complex medication regimens, and the heartbreaking resignation of those who simply gave up on their treatment. These encounters were emotionally taxing, a constant reminder of the systemic issues that hindered equitable access to healthcare.

Right after graduating from AR College of Pharmacy in India, I landed my first job, excited to finally put my training to use and begin my life as a pharmacist. During this time, I had the opportunity to learn about tablet, capsule, and suspension manufacturing techniques, and the process of compounding various formulations, skills that would become the cornerstone of my career. These products, the *so-called life-saving medications*, often made me wonder how they can save patients' lives. The intricacies of pharmaceutical science fascinated me, fueling my passion to excel. It was tough for me to understand how I would stay in the pharmaceutical manufacturing industry in a closed-door setting, and at the same time, I would be able to do what I want to do as a pharmacist.

Ultimately, my heart was drawn more towards direct patient care. I yearned to bridge the gap between science and human connection, believing that my role extended beyond the walls of the laboratory and closed four walls. One moment that stood out was during my commute to the pharma plant in Chhatral from Ahmedabad, when someone said, "What we make here needs to go to the market and be sold properly by our marketing team—we make the best products." The reality of the comment lingered with me, resonating with my own aspirations to influence change not just through high-quality products but through personal interactions. I decided to apply for a position as a medical sales representative or manager, so I could meet doctors and explain how these medications were made and why they could be trusted to help patients.

My transition from a sterile lab environment to the bustling field of medical sales was an enlightening journey. I still remember those days when I went through three steps of the interview to get into Sun Pharma. It felt like a new chapter was unfolding before me. After I got selected for the special division of Sun Pharma, the cardiac medication division, I was invited to go for training in a five-star hotel. The training was an eye-opener, offering insights into both the science of medicine and the art of persuasion. Getting trained as a sales manager for life-saving cardiac medication and then learning how to present it to doctors became something I truly enjoyed. It pulled my full attention and love toward the field of marketing and sales. I was no longer just another pharmacist; I was a bridge between the lab and the healthcare providers, ensuring that the life-saving drugs reached the patients. The training wasn't only about how to present the product to doctors. It was also about how to sell the story behind the product. That year, beauty pageant contestant Aishwarya Rai won the Miss World title. That underlying theme of grace, elegance, and presentation inspired my approach. I remember one of the trainers said, "Beauty remains beauty, whether it's your product and the content or some very famous multimillion-dollar Pharma company." He meant to say that even though we are a small company, we have the same molecule and the best molecule, so the beauty of the product remains within the beauty. You need to showcase it. That lesson stuck with me. I often try to understand how much that lesson has impacted my journey. I have used this several times during my training and coaching. The training wasn't only about how to present the product to doctors. It was also about how to sell the story behind the product. Over the years, I practiced these skills diligently, cultivating both my knowledge and presentation.

After completing all the training, I was assigned to the Saurashtra territory—a peninsular region along the Arabian Sea in Gujarat, India. This region comprises nearly a third of the state and includes several key districts, such as Rajkot. I was eager to embark on my journey. With my determination and the skills honed from rigorous training, I felt prepared to face the challenges ahead. The prospect of exploring new territories excited me. Now I'm in a completely different territory from my hometown, where I was born. The culture is different, but I'm excited and happy to try new foods and learn about the local traditions as I apply marketing and sales strategies to gain momentum. Each day brought new experiences, enriching my understanding and deepening my appreciation for the region.

In Rajkot, I had Penda (a treat I'm still fond of today) - the Siya Ram Penda. This sweet, with its unique taste and texture, quickly became a favorite. And in the morning, the savory Ganthiya & Sambharo became my go-to breakfast. One thing I learned in Rajkot is that from 1 PM to 4 PM, nobody works. It's a time reserved for leisure and rest, a custom deeply ingrained in local culture. During that time, I started meeting different sales representatives, learning how they've been doing their sales and marketing, and picking up tricks of the trade. I observed their strategies, dissecting their approaches bit by bit. I took these learnings to heart, adapting and incorporating them into my methods. This reminds me of a true incident where one of the Pharma Wholesalers in Rajkot recognized that I was new in the field and offered me some valuable lessons, not just in business, but in going out of your way to help someone without expecting anything in return. He told me it always comes back to you in unexpected ways. This philosophy resonated with me and became a part of my own business ethics. The wholesaler's kindness left a lasting impression on me, reinforcing the belief that genuine connections and goodwill transcended mere transactions.

From that town to nearby others, I gradually gained a foothold in pharmaceutical sales management. Early mornings and late nights became familiar companions as I navigated the bustling world of entrepreneurship. While building my network, I discovered the intricate dance of supply and demand and the subtle art of persuasion essential in this field. As a pharmacist, I could communicate more effectively with doctors and better understand their approach to patient care, particularly their reliance on quality pharmaceutical companies. With each encounter, my confidence grew, and I continued to refine my skills as both a territory manager and a pharmacist.

Every few months, I would return to my hometown to visit family. My dad didn't always like what I was doing; he believed I could do more. Yet I understood his perspective and took it in stride. During this time at Sun Pharma, I rented a single room with a kind family in Rajkot. Having my scooter made navigating the town easier, and the family treated me as one of their own, sharing meals and stories that made me feel at home despite being far from mine.

From Rajkot to Junagadh, Porbandar, Jetpur, and many other towns, I had the opportunity to meet so many doctors and pharmacy store owners. It reached a point where, with everything I had learned, like being punctual, writing reports, and organizing myself through a team leader, I started to feel a bit restless and thought I needed to do something different and move up to a management position. So, after working for about a year or so and becoming the highest sales-achieving team leader and doing some crazy numbers in sales, I was awarded a silver coin of Sun Pharma, which I still keep in my prayer box dedicated to the goddess of wealth. Proud of my achievement, I realized it was time to evolve. Embracing change, I decided to enroll in a management training program. And right after that, I joined Samir Remedies and became a Product Training Manager at 24. It was a pivotal moment in my career. My job was to train a former sales representative, and I met Dr. Agarwal. He became my mentor. I started traveling all over India, training sales reps in many different states. The first few months were challenging, adapting to new cultures and expectations across diverse regions. It felt like a fresh start, and I got my own office in Ahmedabad on CG Road. I decorated the office with motivational posters and colorful plants, creating a welcoming space for my trainees. I still do that at age 52. Those who know me and have been to my office this year might have seen it.

As the years passed, my reputation continued to grow, and so did my responsibilities. While I was getting trained as a product manager by Dr. Agarwal, I gained valuable insights, not just about pharmaceuticals, but also about leadership and management. Interacting with Dr. Agarwal broadened my understanding of pharmaceuticals and enhanced my leadership skills. His guidance was invaluable, teaching me to appreciate the balance between empathy and efficiency in managing a team. Under his mentorship, I became more confident and innovative. As the youngest manager in Dr. Agrawal's team, I learned how to deliver the pharmacist's point of view to my team and the sales team. It was an honor to train professionals who were nearly twice my age at the time. Their experience was vast, yet they also valued my fresh insights and energy. Navigating these dynamics taught me the importance of respect and humility—qualities that have since defined my approach to leadership.

There were moments when I wondered whether they were getting and acknowledging what this young 24-year-old pharmacist had to say. Yet, their willingness to listen and engage was a testament to the strength of collaborative learning across generations. I remember this true incident that happened when I was in Patna, the capital of Bihar (a state in eastern India). Ashok, a 56-year-old senior sales rep, secured the job he needed badly to support his family. While I was conducting training, I started having breakfast with him. During those seven days of training, by the third day, I had gotten to know him a little better, and he began opening up about his health issues, especially his diabetes. His honesty and vulnerability allowed us to bridge the gap between age and experience. During that time, I was able to speak as a pharmacist about how amazing it would be if he balanced his diet and, at the same time, did the work he needed to do as a sales rep and fed the family. I felt like I was advising someone twice my age, but it was incredibly rewarding to have that conversation with him. The very next day, when I saw too much Indian bread (roti) on his plate, I smiled and told him, "That's too many layers of diabetes," with a smiley face, and he immediately took out 2 pieces. He smiled back, removed two pieces, and I encouraged him to add some protein. I felt a bit bad, so I got him a small piece of sweet as a reward. Ashok and I stayed in touch even after training was over. He would call me occasionally at headquarters, where I was posted, just to say thank you. Not only did he express his gratitude, but he also went on to become one of the top performers in the company. During one such call, Ashok shared that his improved health had infused new energy into his life.

As I was settling into this new job and no longer traveling as much, a new and very important chapter began in my life. It was time for me to get married. I'd always had an ambitious heart and mind, dreaming of going abroad to settle as a pharmacist for many reasons. One of the biggest reasons was the love and respect I had for the pharmacy profession. And then I got to know more about Asha, now my wife, and an even better pharmacist than me. So many countless memories were made, as life was about to take a turn in a new direction. Asha and I shared a deep connection, one that was built on mutual respect for our profession and a love that transcended boundaries. There's one woman I'll never forget. She was middle-aged, diabetic, and came in regularly. You could see the exhaustion on her face. She couldn't afford her insulin, relying instead on rationing her limited supply. I vividly remember her pleading look, the desperation in her voice as she explained her predicament. Even though my role as a pharmacist was limited, I did whatever I could, looking into discount programs, cheaper brands, and any workaround I could find. In the end, I found a program that offered some relief, but the experience left an indelible mark on my heart, solidifying my commitment to addressing healthcare disparities. Another memorable case involved a young mother who struggled to afford medication for her asthmatic child. The medication was crucial for managing the child's condition, yet the cost was beyond the family's reach. The desperation in the mother's eyes was palpable. She talked about how bad her child's condition got when she couldn't afford the inhaler, and I could tell she was holding herself together just long enough to ask for help. This incident triggered in me an even stronger desire to help underserved communities, to create a system that could provide access to life-saving medications for everyone, regardless of their ability to pay. Sometimes, the effects of my work were visible in multiple generations. I remember working one evening at Bayshore Home Care Pharmacy when a woman named Susan came in. She needed a nebulizer. I opened the box myself and showed her how to use it, whether or not it was covered. Susan had tears in her eyes when she realized her child could finally breathe without that constant fear.

Fast forward about 15 to 17 years, I hired a young girl to work as a clerk in my pharmacy, and guess what? That girl was the patient. It was Susan's daughter, Emily. Now grown up, she wanted to give back to the community that had once come to her aid. She was going to Brookdale Community College for undergraduate studies and, at the same time, wanted to learn more about pharmacy. Emily's presence was a reminder of the impact that compassion and support could have on people's lives.

My early career was a period of rapid learning and profound emotional growth. I had to adjust to the reality of practice, figuring out how insurance actually worked, and dealing with the emotional side of being the person patients turned to when they couldn't afford their meds. It was in those early years, however, that the seeds of my future vision for a charitable pharmacy began to take root.

Every shift showed me how uneven healthcare access really was and how much-underserved communities were struggling. It made me realize that someone had to step up.

It wasn't just about money either. I met so many patients who didn't understand how or when to take their meds. Many simply couldn't understand their complex treatment plans, resulting in missed doses, ineffective treatment, and a cycle of worsening health conditions. These instances highlighted the significant communication gap between healthcare providers and patients, a gap that often went unaddressed in the fast-paced, high-volume environment of a retail pharmacy. I realized that effective healthcare wasn't merely about dispensing medications; it was about patient education, understanding their individual needs and challenges, and creating a collaborative approach to care. This realization solidified my commitment to not just providing medications but also providing comprehensive patient care, including education and counseling.

Of course, working with the healthcare system came with its own set of battles. Insurance paperwork, prior authorizations, and endless rules about what was covered often created frustrating barriers between patients and the medications they needed. I spent countless hours on the phone with insurance companies, fighting for approvals and explaining the medical necessity of certain prescriptions. These encounters were often time-consuming and emotionally draining, but essential in ensuring that patients received the care they deserved.

These experiences deepened my drive to find better, simpler ways to get medications to people who couldn't afford them or didn't know how to work through the complicated healthcare system.

The experiences of my early career were tough, no doubt, but they were also some of the most fulfilling moments of my life. I still remember the way a patient's shoulders would drop in relief when I managed to get their medication secured. Or how their eyes lit up just because I took the time to explain things properly. And the subtle shifts in their demeanor as they began to regain control over their health condition. These personal connections, even if fleeting in the context of a busy retail environment, affirmed my decision to pursue a career dedicated to improving the health and well-being of the community. And the more I saw how much even a small effort could mean to someone, the more I felt pulled toward the deeper purpose of it all.

The hard truth about healthcare inequality hit me all at once. It wasn't something I slowly came to understand, it landed like a punch to the chest. My retail pharmacy, nestled in a low-income neighborhood, became a clear window into a much bigger problem. I saw it in the anxious faces of patients struggling to decipher complex insurance forms, the palpable desperation in the eyes of those who couldn't afford their life-saving medications, and the quiet resignation of those who had simply given up hope.

One instance stands out, etched in my memory with the clarity of a photograph. Mr. Henderson, a frail elderly man with a history of heart failure, relied on a daily cocktail of medications to keep his condition under control. He always walked in slowly, his hands trembling as he pulled his worn-out wallet from his coat. He would carefully count out each bill and coin, his movements slow and deliberate, each transaction a testament to the immense financial strain he was under. His medications were essential for his survival, yet their cost threatened to consume his limited resources. He frequently arrived at the pharmacy with a hesitant approach, his eyes darting nervously as if anticipating a negative outcome. The fear of not being able to afford his life-sustaining medication was almost as palpable as the symptoms of his illness.

Another patient, a young mother named Maria, showed me just how hard working families had it, trying to care for their kids while barely scraping by. Maria worked tirelessly as a cleaner, juggling two jobs to make ends meet, but still couldn't always afford the inhalers her son Miguel needed for his asthma. Whenever she had to skip filling the prescription, Miguel's asthma attacks would spike, a painful reminder of how deeply financial stress affects health. Maria's story became emblematic of the countless families I encountered, constantly wrestling with the agonizing decision of prioritizing essential needs and medications over other necessities. The weight of this responsibility was evident in the lines of worry permanently etched on her face and in the tired droop of her shoulders.

These weren't isolated incidents. Day after day, I witnessed patients forced to make choices no one should have to make. I saw patients forgoing meals to afford their medications, delaying necessary medical appointments due to transportation costs, and sacrificing other essentials to prioritize their health needs. These were not abstract statistics; these were real people, with real lives, facing real struggles. Their experiences shattered my idealized image of a healthcare system that provided equal access to all.

Beyond the financial barriers, I met patients who struggled with just understanding their medications. Many lacked the health literacy to understand their medications, dosage instructions, or potential side effects. The fast-paced environment of a retail pharmacy often didn't allow for the necessary time to provide thorough patient education. These individuals were often left to navigate their treatment plans alone, frequently resulting in missed doses, adverse reactions, and ultimately, poor health outcomes. The lack of sufficient patient education, which usually came down to time and staff shortages, highlighted a significant flaw in our system. The system prioritized speed and volume, but that meant patients often walked away confused and alone.

The bureaucratic obstacles posed by insurance companies added another layer of complexity to an already difficult situation. Trying to deal with prior authorizations, restrictive formularies, and surprise denials became part of my daily routine. I spent countless hours on the phone, advocating for my patients, trying to overcome the systemic barriers that stood between them and the medications they desperately needed. The constant frustration of dealing with insurance companies, compounded by the urgency of the patients' needs, weighed heavily on my mind. The sheer number of forms, approvals, and endless loops of paperwork was overwhelming.

The complexity created needless anxiety, often exacerbating patients' stress levels and undermining their well-being. The system may have been built for efficiency on the insurer's end, but for the people relying on it, it felt like being constantly pushed aside.

Chapter 2: Seva in Action: A Lifelong Commitment to Indian Health Camp of New Jersey

It wasn't part of the prescription. It wasn't written in any textbook.

But it was one of the most rewarding experiences of my life as a pharmacist.

That day, I realized: true care is not bound by job descriptions or pharmacy walls.

It's about seeing the patient beyond the prescription — about becoming a source of comfort, humanity, and dignity when they need it the most.

Moments like these reminded me why I chose this path — and why, eventually, I was called to create something even greater: a place where service, compassion, and healing could live together under one roof, without barriers.

Because healing isn't just about medicine, it's about kindness in action, not my action, but it was an action of a caring pharmacist. Kudos to all those pharmacists who do this each and every day! They quietly make a difference, transforming the lives they touch, one thoughtful gesture at a time.

When I think about the true meaning of Seva — selfless service — my heart immediately returns to the Indian Health Camp of New Jersey.

I first joined the Indian Health Camp family around 2003–2004, alongside an extraordinary team led by Dr. Tushar Patel. Back then, I was a young pharmacist, still shaping my understanding of how much one person could give beyond the counter, beyond the clinic. Every year, we hosted three to four free health camps across New Jersey, offering medical, dental, vision, and pharmacy services at no cost to patients, many of whom had no insurance, no resources, and nowhere else to turn. For me, providing pharmacy services wasn't just about handing out medications. It was about giving dignity to someone who felt forgotten, restoring hope where there was fear, and seeing the light return to someone's eyes as it ignited something deeper inside my own heart. I had the extreme honor of supplying free medications to countless patients during those camps—people who otherwise would have had to choose between paying for medicine or paying for food. I'll never forget one particular lady who suffered from severe incontinence. We were able to provide her with much-needed adult diapers, completely free of charge. The gratitude and blessings in her eyes were more valuable than any paycheck or recognition. Those silent, tearful blessings touched my soul in ways words never could.

Over the past twenty years, the Indian Health Camp became more than just an event I participated in—it became part of who I am. Today, I am humbled to serve as a proud member of its Board of Trustees, working alongside others who believe, like I do, that true healing begins with compassion, service, and love. One of the proudest moments of my Seva journey was bringing my son, Sarthak, to a health camp. I wanted him to see, firsthand, what Seva looked like—not just in theory, but in action. I wanted him to understand the words of Mahatma Gandhi: "The best way to find yourself is to lose yourself in the service of others." Watching Sarthak absorb those lessons not in a classroom, but in real life, was one of the greatest gifts I could give him as a father.

And it reminded me once again: service is not just about changing lives—it's about letting service change you. The transformation is mutual, a dance of give and take, where the giver receives as much as they provide.

***

Saving a Life: The Moment That Redefined My Role. As pharmacists, we often stand behind the counter filling prescriptions, counseling patients, and checking drug interactions, but very few people truly understand the gravity of the trust placed in our hands.

On that afternoon of February 8th, 2017, in my DrugSmart Pharmacy in Keansburg, that trust was tested in the most profound way, and it changed me forever.

When Katrina Thompson walked into the store, something about her wasn't right.

It wasn't just a clinical observation; it was the deep connection that only comes from truly knowing your patients. Her face, her posture, the way she struggled to speak, it triggered every instinct inside me.

When I took her blood pressure, my heart sank. 43 over 32.

Numbers that most textbooks would call incompatible with life.

At that moment, the room stood still. There was no time for hesitation. There was only time for action.

I remembered what I was taught in pharmacy school — about how salt can temporarily lift dangerously low blood pressure. We rushed to get her salt, kept her talking, kept her awake, kept fighting for her to stay conscious.

I remember telling her, "Please stay with us. Don't go to sleep. You'll go into a coma."

And all I could think was — this is someone's daughter. This is someone's mother, someone's sister... and right now, she's depending on me.

It was one of the most humbling, terrifying, and rewarding experiences of my life.

Later, when I found out that Katrina had a pulmonary embolism — a blood clot in her lung — I realized just how critical those minutes were.

Had she gone home, had she collapsed alone, had she not made it to us in time... the outcome could have been devastating.

In that moment, I realized that being a pharmacist is about so much more than prescriptions.

It's about presence. It's about vigilance. It's about purpose.

Even now, thinking back to that day, I feel a deep sense of gratitude that I was there, that I had the knowledge, and that I could make a difference when it mattered most.

Saving a life humbles you.

It reminds you why you chose this path. It grounds you in service. It anchors you back to your Seva, your calling.

Katrina's story isn't just about what I did for her. It's about what she gave me:

A living reminder that every patient, every moment, every heartbeat matters.

The Day a Blood Pressure Reading Changed Everything. Salt, Faith, and a Life Saved.

***

World's Greatest Pharmacist: A Moment of True Reward - A Christmas Ornament Gift

December 9, 2019 — It was an ordinary, busy day at Bayshore Homecare Pharmacy in Holmdel.

The phone was ringing, insurance claims were being rejected left and right, and like always, I was doing everything I could to help patients — even when the system made it hard.

I was filling prescriptions that barely paid for the cost of the medicine, let alone the time, energy, and care we poured into every single prescription.

But none of that mattered to me. What mattered was the person on the other side — the patient who was trusting me to be there for them.

That day, without any expectation, I was handed a Christmas ornament.

It said:

"World's Greatest Pharmacist - Ritesh." - I still have this on my desk.

It wasn't about the money.

It wasn't about the numbers.

It wasn't even about the pharmacy.

It was about the simple truth:

When you serve from your heart, people feel it. And sometimes, they send that love right back to you in ways you never expect.

That ornament reminded me why I chose this path.

It wasn't for recognition. It was for moments like this — when someone, quietly and sincerely, tells you:

"You made a difference in my life."

And that… is a reward no paycheck could ever match.

From Pharmacist to CEO — Purpose in Every Role

After dedicating nearly two decades as a frontline pharmacist across New Jersey, my journey evolved into something even greater in May 2019, when I took on the role of CEO of Legacy Pharmacy Group. It was a humbling milestone — a culmination of years spent not just dispensing medications, but building relationships, saving lives, and making a difference one patient at a time. My foundation was not built in boardrooms — it was built behind pharmacy counters, at health fairs, and on the frontlines of community care.

Throughout those twenty years, my role as a pharmacist went far beyond filling prescriptions. I found deep purpose in volunteering my time and expertise at places like the Indian Health Camp of New Jersey, where we provided essential health services at no cost to underserved populations.

Serving alongside dedicated physicians like Dr. Tushar Patel and countless volunteers taught me the true meaning of Seva — selfless service. I also contributed to the Erskine Foundation, providing education and care to diabetic patients, where again, the mission was clear: to give back, to educate, and to uplift.

Along the way, I was blessed to receive recognition that honored these efforts — being named Pharmacist of the Year, earning community service awards, and being acknowledged for my contribution to public health. But even as these accolades arrived, I always felt that the true reward was invisible: it lived in the smiles, the thank-yous, the lives touched quietly without any headlines or fanfare. Service was — and remains — its own greatest reward.

Just as I stepped into my new leadership role in 2019, the world changed overnight. COVID-19 stormed into our lives in early 2020, and every plan, every business strategy, suddenly became secondary to a single, urgent mission: saving lives. I vividly remember the day we hosted our first Zoom call to rally pharmacists across New Jersey. Over 100 pharmacists joined — so many that the platform crashed. That crash wasn't a failure; it was proof that we were united by something bigger than ourselves. The Inner Pharmacist — the healer, the protector, the servant leader — woke up inside all of us.

Innovation became the lifeline. Working closely with legislators, I helped pioneer new methods for COVID-19 specimen collection, testing, and later, vaccination administration. It was not just about adapting; it was about leading. With the help of my wife and my incredible team, we carried out millions of COVID tests between 2020 and 2022. I still remember standing in full protective gear, collecting specimens at Elizabeth Dunn Center, mixing vaccines to prepare for mass vaccination drives, and making sure every vial, every dose, every swab served its sacred purpose: to protect a life.

But it wasn't without heartbreak. During those years, we witnessed a profound loss of friends, family, colleagues, and patients. Each life lost carved another scar in our hearts. Yet amidst the grief, a renewed sense of purpose was born.

Being a pharmacist was never just a job; it was a calling. The pandemic stripped away titles and positions and reminded all of us of the raw humanity at the core of our profession. Through those years of chaos, my commitment only deepened: to always serve with compassion, to always innovate in crisis, and to always stand ready for those who need us most.

During the darkest months of the pandemic, innovation and collaboration became the light we all desperately needed. As CEO of Legacy Pharmacy Group and still a pharmacist at heart, I was proud to partner with Health Mart to bring COVID-19 specimen collection to several of our Health Mart pharmacies. But the need only kept growing. Working with local laboratories, we quickly expanded our testing efforts across the state, adapting to whatever it took to meet the demand.

Some mornings, in the freezing cold, we stood at train stations in Little Silver and Hazlet, collecting specimens at dawn for commuters heading to work. We set up in schools, in parking lots, anywhere people needed us.

It was during this time that I met Dr. Joseph Howe, a passionate advocate who needed COVID testing services to safely reopen schools in Freehold Borough. Our paths crossed out of necessity, but what grew from it was a bond of brotherhood, built on shared values and purpose. Today, Dr. Howe continues to serve alongside me as a member of the Advisory Board for the Ritesh Shah Charitable Pharmacy.

Similarly, our work at the Elizabeth Dunn Center, side by side with teams of pharmacists and county officials like Ed Oatman from Union County Government, showed me what was possible when public service and private purpose aligned. Every partnership, every early morning test, every sleepless night, it was all a testament to what can happen when you lead with your heart.

During the early days of the pandemic in 2020, life as a pharmacist — and as a husband married to a fellow pharmacist — became something far greater than a profession. It became a calling of the soul. Together, from our own home garage, my wife and I began conducting countless COVID specimen collections. Every morning, before the sun rose, we would receive calls from friends — many of them leaders in government or essential services — who needed testing urgently so they could continue their critical work.

There was no hesitation. We would rush to the pharmacy, sometimes at 5 or 6 a.m., opening the doors before the world even woke up, ready to serve. People came to us with urgent needs — some traveling to say final goodbyes to loved ones, some desperate to protect their families, some clinging to hope in the middle of unbearable loss. In those sacred early hours, amidst the cold and fear, I found my true purpose in life: to heal, to serve, to be there.

Beyond testing, there were battles we fought behind the scenes — like trying to secure protective masks when they were almost impossible to find. I still remember the day we finally managed to import 10,000 three-layer 3M masks to distribute to pharmacy members who were risking their lives serving the public. Within just ten minutes, they were all gone. I stood there, my eyes wide open, realizing the depth of this crisis. Where were we heading as a society? How could we do more to protect our community, to save every precious human life we could reach? That question haunted me and fueled me every day. We worked tirelessly to source the best SARS-CoV-2 Combo Rapid Test Kits, doing everything in our power to make testing accessible, affordable, and reliable to bring a sense of normalcy back to a broken world.

And we did not do it alone. I had the honor of collaborating with leaders like Steve Honigman, who once served under President Clinton, and Senator Vin Gopal, who championed pharmacists by writing an op-ed in the newspaper calling for expanded pharmacist rights during the crisis. Together, we pushed forward, advocating for pharmacists to be recognized for what we truly are: frontline healthcare heroes, trained and trusted to save lives. This was a war without a visible enemy, but in every swab, every mask, every act of compassion, we were quietly fighting back, driven not by profit, but by pure purpose.

Chapter 3 The Pandemic

The initial wave of the pandemic hit us like a tsunami. The carefully laid plans for our charitable pharmacy, still just getting off the ground, were instantly rendered inadequate. The schedules we'd crafted, the workflows we'd mapped out, and the patient projections we'd planned for were all swept away by the sudden, overwhelming surge in demand. The community, already struggling with healthcare disparities, was now facing a crisis of unprecedented proportions. The familiar anxieties about funding and regulatory compliance paled in comparison to the immediate, urgent needs unfolding before us.

Our first challenge was procuring essential medications. The supply chains, already strained, were buckling under the immense pressure. Many medications, particularly those used in the treatment of respiratory illnesses, were suddenly in critically short supply. The pharmaceutical wholesalers, accustomed to predictable demand patterns, were struggling to keep up. Our carefully negotiated contracts, so painstakingly secured, seemed almost irrelevant in this new, volatile landscape. We found ourselves competing not only with other pharmacies but also with hospitals and healthcare systems, all desperately vying for the same limited resources.

The initial panic was palpable. We held emergency meetings late into the night, strategizing, brainstorming, and adapting our protocols. We had to move quickly, decisively, and with a profound sense of urgency. Our team, a small but incredibly dedicated group, worked tirelessly, juggling multiple priorities and making tough decisions under immense pressure.

We shifted from our meticulously crafted launch strategy to a crisis-response mode, adapting to the rapidly changing circumstances.

The first priority was securing a reliable supply of essential medications. We expanded our network of suppliers, exploring alternative sources, negotiating favorable terms, and prioritizing the acquisition of critical medications such as antibiotics, antiviral drugs, and pain relievers. We leveraged our established relationships with local hospitals and healthcare providers, collaborating to identify and address shortages. It was frustrating and draining—countless calls, ignored emails, and the constant fear we'd run out of something vital. But the pressure pushed us to be more resourceful, more collaborative.

Simultaneously, we had to adapt our operational protocols to maintain safety and efficiency. We implemented strict infection control measures, exceeding even the stringent guidelines issued by the public health authorities. This meant procuring personal protective equipment (PPE), training our staff in proper donning and doffing procedures, and reorganizing our workflow to minimize contact between patients and staff. We introduced telehealth consultations, leveraging technology to provide remote medication management and counseling. This was a significant shift, demanding a rapid upskilling of our staff and a significant investment in new technologies.

Beyond the logistical challenges, we faced the emotionally taxing task of serving a community grappling with fear, anxiety, and loss. Many of our patients were elderly, immunocompromised, or otherwise vulnerable, facing heightened risks from the virus. We provided not only medication but also emotional support, acting as a lifeline for those isolated and terrified. Our pharmacists, beyond their professional expertise, offered a listening ear, a reassuring voice, and a steadfast commitment to their well-being. We transformed from simple dispensers of medications into trusted advisors and compassionate caregivers.

One memory that stays with me is of Mrs. Rodriguez, an elderly woman who lived alone and relied on us for her daily meds. When the lockdown began, she became increasingly isolated and afraid. Our team made regular check-in calls, not just to ensure she had her medications but also to inquire about her well-being. We delivered her medications directly to her doorstep, ensuring she had enough food and essential supplies. These seemingly small gestures went a long way in alleviating her anxiety and loneliness, reminding her that she wasn't alone in this crisis.

The experience underscored the importance of community engagement. We partnered with local food banks, social service agencies, and community groups to coordinate efforts and reach those most vulnerable. This collaboration proved invaluable in identifying and assisting individuals and families struggling to access healthcare and essential resources. The strength of our response wasn't simply our ingenuity or resilience; it was the power of collective action, the shared commitment to serving those in dire need.

The pandemic forced us to confront our own limitations and biases. We realized that our meticulously planned strategies, while well-intentioned, were not enough to address the complex and rapidly evolving nature of a public health crisis. We learned the importance of flexibility, adaptability, and rapid response. We learned to embrace uncertainty, to acknowledge our limitations, and to rely on the strength of our team and our community partners.

Another pivotal aspect of our response was addressing the misinformation and fear surrounding the virus. We became active disseminators of accurate information, providing patients with reliable sources of information, debunking myths, and dispelling anxieties. Our pharmacists were on the front lines, answering questions, providing clear and concise information, and combating the spread of misinformation that could have had life-threatening consequences. This involved continuous education of our team and ourselves, staying updated on the rapidly changing guidelines and recommendations. We had to sift through a mountain of data, isolate the valid information, and present it in a clear, understandable way.

The challenges were immense. The emotional toll was heavy. Yet, our dedication to our community and our commitment to our mission kept us going. We celebrated small victories – securing a shipment of urgently needed medications, securing a new source for PPE, and developing a successful telehealth program. These milestones, while seemingly insignificant in the grand scheme of things, were crucial in bolstering our morale, reinforcing our belief in our cause, and driving us forward.

The pandemic really pushed us to our limits. It tested our resilience, forced us to get creative, and made us question how prepared we really were. It showed us just how fragile our healthcare system is and how many people fall through the cracks when things go wrong. We had to face some hard truths about inequality in healthcare and how urgently we need to fix it.

But through it all, we also saw something powerful. We saw our community come together. We saw our team show up, day after day, with compassion and determination. We weren't just reacting to a crisis; we were growing through it. And somehow, even in the middle of the chaos, we became stronger. We learned more than we ever expected, and that experience will shape how we move forward. We're now more committed than ever to making healthcare accessible, kind, and fair for everyone.

The pandemic, as awful as it was, pushed us to rethink how we work. It made us more open to new ideas, more willing to lean on each other, and more focused on why our pharmacy exists in the first place — to help people who need it most.

The constant pressure meant we had to change fast. We had to stop worrying about long-term plans and focus on what could save lives right now. That meant putting our educational programs and outreach on hold for a while. All that mattered was helping people get through the next day.

The immediate need was to save lives, and that became our singular, unwavering focus. We developed a tiered system for prioritizing patients, designating those with the most urgent needs – those facing life-threatening conditions exacerbated by the pandemic – as the highest priority. This meant readily available antibiotics for severe bacterial infections, antiviral medications for those severely impacted by influenza or other viral illnesses, and the necessary pain management for individuals with chronic conditions struggling to access their usual care.

One case that stands out involved a young mother, Sarah, who contracted pneumonia shortly after giving birth prematurely. The hospital, overwhelmed by COVID-19 patients, was struggling to provide adequate care. Sarah's condition was deteriorating rapidly, and the lack of readily available intensive care beds meant that her survival was far from certain. We stepped in, working closely with the hospital's medical team to ensure Sarah had access to the necessary antibiotics and other supportive medications. We also coordinated home healthcare visits to support her and her baby, providing necessary medications and monitoring her progress. Thanks to this collaborative effort, Sarah made a full recovery, allowing her to return home to her newborn child. This intervention underscores the pivotal role we played not just in providing medications but in bridging critical gaps in the overwhelmed healthcare system.

Another powerful example involved Mr. Jones, an elderly man with a history of heart failure. His regular medications were suddenly unavailable due to supply chain disruptions. His condition worsened dramatically, and without access to his life-saving medications, his life was at serious risk. Our team, through tireless searching and networking with various pharmaceutical distributors and even making appeals to other pharmacy networks, located a small, emergency supply of his medication from a smaller independent distributor located several states away. We arranged for overnight courier delivery and personally ensured Mr. Jones received the medication in time. The quick response likely saved his life and highlighted our resourcefulness and dedication to going the extra mile to save lives. We learned early on that "conventional" solutions often didn't work, requiring us to explore unconventional and creative ways of accessing life-saving drugs.

The pandemic also highlighted the pre-existing health inequities within our community. We noticed that access to essential medications and healthcare services was disproportionately affected among low-income communities and communities of color. Many individuals lacked access to transportation, internet, or even basic healthcare literacy, significantly hampering their ability to navigate the healthcare system during a pandemic. This disparity led us to further expand our community partnerships. We collaborated with local churches, community centers, and social service organizations to create mobile medication distribution points in underserved neighborhoods. These outreach initiatives, often involving our own staff volunteering their time, ensured that vulnerable populations had easy access to essential medications and health information. We made conscious decisions to prioritize underserved populations. We allocated a certain percentage of our limited resources to these communities, recognizing that systemic inequalities often put them at greater risk.

Beyond the immediate provision of medications, we realized the vital importance of providing comprehensive patient support. This included coordinating transportation to healthcare facilities, providing referrals to mental health services, and offering support with obtaining essential supplies like food and personal protective equipment. We actively engaged with public health officials to disseminate accurate and reliable information about the virus and debunk widespread misinformation that was both frightening and dangerous to our community.

The experience of delivering medication and crucial healthcare services to people in vulnerable situations wasn't merely logistical; it was deeply personal. We formed lasting connections with patients, families, and healthcare professionals. In many cases, we became a source of comfort and reassurance during a time of widespread fear and uncertainty. We witnessed the profound impact of human compassion and the power of collaboration in overcoming seemingly insurmountable challenges. Our efforts weren't just about dispensing pills; they were about offering hope and a lifeline.

Another case that stays with us is Maria's. She was a single mother with three young kids who lost her job during the early lockdowns. She'd already been struggling to afford her diabetes medication, and the pandemic made things even worse. Through our network, we helped her connect with a local food bank and gave her financial help to cover her medication costs. This wraparound support helped her stay healthy so she could continue caring for her children. Maria's story reminded us how important it is to look at the full picture when helping someone. We need to go beyond prescriptions and consider the real-life challenges that affect a person's health.

This experience of addressing the pandemic wasn't without significant challenges. We had to overcome bureaucratic hurdles, navigate complex supply chains, and constantly adapt to the rapidly changing circumstances. There were moments of immense pressure, feelings of frustration, and the sheer exhaustion that comes from working tirelessly under stressful conditions. However, what stood out throughout was the unwavering commitment of our team.

Their dedication, compassion, and problem-solving skills were truly exceptional, consistently exceeding expectations.

We developed a robust system for tracking patients and their medication needs, ensuring that those with the highest levels of risk were identified and prioritized. We utilized technology extensively, deploying telehealth platforms for remote patient monitoring, medication counseling, and even initial triage.

This approach mitigated infection risks, improved access to care, and allowed us to efficiently manage our resources.

This was a huge step forward, and it's a testament to our willingness to adapt and evolve our approach.

Looking back, it's clear that our response to the pandemic involved more than just dispensing medications. We became a critical pillar of the community support system. We provided life-saving interventions, bridged healthcare gaps, and empowered people to navigate this incredibly challenging period. What we learned during this intense period will be invaluable as we continue to develop our charitable pharmacy and serve our community. This experience taught us the importance of not only having well-defined strategies but also the ability to adapt and overcome unexpected hurdles. The pandemic, while devastating, served as a potent catalyst for growth and innovation. It highlighted the profound impact a community pharmacy, with a strong focus on patient care and community engagement, can have in improving public health. It also emphasized that our mission goes far beyond the mere dispensing of medication; it's about saving lives, providing hope, and building a healthier, more equitable community.

The pandemic forced us to reconsider the very definition of our role as pharmacists. While dispensing medications remained central, it became increasingly clear that our impact extended far beyond the pharmacy counter. The sheer scale of the crisis necessitated a shift from individual patient care to a broader, community-focused approach. This meant building bridges—strong, resilient bridges—connecting disparate elements of our community to ensure equitable access to healthcare and essential resources.

One of the most important bridges we built was with the local hospital system. Before the pandemic, our interactions were limited to routine exchanges; we filled prescriptions, answered questions, and provided routine medication counseling. The pandemic transformed this relationship. We found ourselves working hand-in-hand with hospital administrators, nurses, and doctors, sharing real-time information on medication availability, coordinating patient transfers, and even providing emergency medication deliveries to patients discharged prematurely to alleviate pressure on hospital beds. This collaboration, born out of necessity, fostered a level of trust and mutual respect that continues to this day. We created a streamlined communication system, utilizing secure messaging platforms and regular conference calls to ensure efficient information sharing and coordinated care. This system enabled us to rapidly respond to changing needs, adapt to evolving guidelines, and anticipate potential shortages of essential medications.

Our partnership with the local health department proved equally vital. We became a key channel for sharing trustworthy information about the virus, correcting false claims, and educating our community on how to protect themselves and others. We actively participated in public health campaigns, handing out educational materials, running vaccination clinics at our pharmacy, and even organizing virtual sessions to reach more people. This involved not only providing factual information but also addressing the emotional toll of the pandemic, offering reassurance and support to a community grappling with fear and uncertainty. This collaboration underscored the importance of simple, clear communication during a public health emergency, particularly within underserved communities where misinformation often proliferated. We focused our outreach efforts on ensuring that culturally appropriate and linguistically accessible information was readily available. We translated key materials into several languages, partnering with community organizations to disseminate information effectively. We also made a conscious decision to target messaging on the platforms used most often by our diverse communities. This showed that providing information alone was not enough, but actively reaching the community was also imperative.

Beyond the formal partnerships, we saw a beautiful wave of community-led efforts. Volunteers from local churches, schools, and community groups stepped forward, offering their time and resources. We collaborated with these volunteers to establish mobile medication delivery services, ensuring that homebound individuals and those lacking transportation had access to their prescriptions. These volunteers became an invaluable extension of our team, providing not only medication delivery but also friendly companionship and a much-needed sense of connection during a time of isolation. Moreover, these volunteers frequently became a link between the patient and us, relaying crucial information about medication adherence, side effects, and other important concerns. This mutual exchange of knowledge and care highlighted the power of community involvement and the effectiveness of collaborative efforts.

We formalized these collaborations by creating a volunteer management system, providing training on medication handling and safety protocols, and implementing a robust communication network.

The challenges, of course, were significant. Supply chain disruptions led to shortages of essential medications, forcing us to employ creative solutions such as sourcing medications from alternative suppliers, negotiating with wholesalers, and even reaching out to other pharmacies across the state for assistance. We developed a sophisticated inventory management system, utilizing real-time data to track medication availability and anticipate potential shortages. We also explored alternative treatment options and explored ways to safely utilize generic equivalents where appropriate. These flexible approaches kept us going. The sheer number of patients needing help, combined with the risk of infection, stretched us thin. But the dedication of our team and the generosity of our community partners kept us moving forward.

Many of us worked long hours, often putting aside our own well-being to make sure patients got the care they needed. That shared sense of purpose kept us grounded and helped reduce burnout during the most difficult moments.

The pandemic also exacerbated pre-existing health inequities within our community. We recognized the disproportionate impact on low-income families and communities of color, who often faced significant barriers to accessing healthcare. We partnered with local social service agencies to identify and assist these vulnerable populations. This involved not only providing medication access but also addressing social determinants of health, such as food insecurity, housing instability, and lack of transportation. We worked closely with community leaders and healthcare professionals to assess the unique needs of these communities, tailoring our support programs to address the specific challenges they faced.

We partnered with organizations that provided food assistance, housing assistance, and transportation, as well as mental health support. This holistic approach was critical in providing effective care and improving health outcomes for vulnerable groups. This collaborative approach showcased the effectiveness of partnerships that go beyond providing medication to address comprehensive health needs.

Building these bridges wasn't just about logistics; it was about fostering trust and empathy. We became not only healthcare providers but also sources of comfort, offering emotional support and being there to listen to patients and families who were overwhelmed with anxiety and fear. The relationships we built during this time were deep and lasting, strengthening our ties to the community and reinforcing our dedication to patient-centered care. These experiences strengthened the emotional connections and built trust with our community, resulting in greater patient engagement and better adherence to treatment plans. The human aspect of the collaborations formed during the pandemic helped make it easier for patients to trust us and feel more comfortable seeking help.

These connections transcended the traditional pharmacist-patient interactions and built strong links with our community. The resilience and strength displayed by both our team and our community partners during the pandemic provided invaluable insights into the importance of collaborative community efforts in addressing challenging issues in public health.

Looking back, the pandemic's crucible forged a stronger, more resilient community. The bridges we built among healthcare workers, community groups, and individuals are still standing, showing us the strength of compassion, cooperation, and a shared purpose in advancing public health. The lessons we learned about adaptability, resourcefulness, and the vital importance of community engagement will continue to guide our efforts as we move forward. The experience not only shaped our pharmacy's approach to patient care but also strengthened our commitment to building community and working collaboratively in healthcare. We learned how collaborative partnerships could amplify our reach and impact, particularly the importance of building relationships proactively, not only reacting to crises. This ongoing commitment to community engagement remains a cornerstone of our philosophy and practice. It has elevated our role beyond dispensing medications, making us a valuable asset to our community's overall health and well-being.

The pandemic's impact extended far beyond the immediate health crisis; it exposed the fragility of our healthcare supply chain, leaving us grappling with unprecedented shortages of essential medications and medical supplies. This wasn't simply a matter of empty shelves; it was a direct threat to the health and well-being of our most vulnerable patients. The initial weeks were marked by a scramble for basic necessities – face masks, hand sanitizer, and, most critically, medications to treat COVID-19 and existing chronic conditions.

Our regular suppliers couldn't keep up, deliveries became unreliable, and many items were simply out of stock. We saw how one missing ingredient could stop the production of several medications, triggering widespread shortages. The situation was particularly acute for medications requiring specialized manufacturing processes or relying on raw materials sourced from overseas. For example, the reliance on certain countries for the production of key active pharmaceutical ingredients (APIs) exposed the vulnerabilities within a globalized supply chain. The sudden halt in international trade and transportation created significant delays and shortages that directly affected our ability to provide essential medications. We saw delays in the delivery of common antibiotics, pain relievers, and even insulin, life-sustaining treatments for many.

Our response involved a multifaceted approach, fueled by a determination. First, we ramped up our efforts to predict demand more accurately, using real-time data from electronic health records and reviewing past prescription patterns. This allowed us to proactively identify potential shortages and adjust our ordering strategies accordingly. We started ordering larger quantities of items anticipated to be in short supply, strategically building up our inventory where possible. This proactive approach proved crucial in mitigating the impact of disruptions on patient care, but it demanded careful consideration of storage space and medication expiration dates. This was a careful balancing act, requiring constant monitoring and precise inventory management.

Next, we diversified our supply chain, actively seeking alternative suppliers both domestically and internationally. This involved extensive research, contacting numerous wholesalers and manufacturers, and meticulously evaluating their reliability and compliance standards. Building these new partnerships wasn't easy; it required navigating complex logistical challenges and establishing trust with unfamiliar suppliers, a process demanding both patience and persistence. This expanded network provided essential redundancy, allowing us to circumvent shortages in certain regions by accessing supplies from other locations. We even established direct relationships with some manufacturers to secure supplies more efficiently, bypassing the traditional wholesale channels. The process was lengthy and complex, but in the long run, it strengthened our resilience and mitigated future potential disruptions.

The challenges weren't solely limited to procuring medication; securing essential personal protective equipment (PPE) for our staff also presented significant hurdles. Early in the pandemic, procuring N95 masks, gloves, and gowns was a Herculean task. We collaborated with local businesses, hospitals, and community groups to secure supplies, often relying on mutual aid networks and creative solutions. We even joined forces with a local seamstress who repurposed fabric to create cloth face masks for our staff, illustrating how community cooperation can make a tangible difference.

Securing appropriate PPE not only protected our staff but also ensured the continuity of our services, allowing us to continue providing essential care to our patients.

At the same time, we were facing another pressing challenge: ensuring fair access to limited resources. We knew that certain groups — like seniors, people with chronic conditions, and families living paycheck to paycheck — were hit hardest by the shortages. They didn't always have the tools or means to navigate a complicated healthcare system. So we partnered with community clinics, social service agencies, and nonprofits to find out who needed help most and make sure those individuals came first. We built systems to flag high-priority prescriptions, ensuring patients with urgent needs got their medications without delay. We also expanded our mobile delivery services to reach people who were homebound or without transportation.

This approach wasn't just practical, it was ethical. We knew that doing things fairly meant looking beyond availability and making decisions based on actual patient needs.

The situation also required innovative problem-solving, prompting us to explore alternative treatment options and utilize generic equivalents wherever possible. We collaborated with physicians to review patient treatment plans, identifying situations where generic medications could be safely substituted, alleviating some pressure on the supply chain. This involved continuous communication with physicians to ensure that medication changes were made safely and appropriately, preserving the integrity of patient care. We also expanded our role beyond traditional dispensing, providing comprehensive medication counseling and helping patients understand their medications and manage their conditions effectively.

On top of all this, the pandemic highlighted the crucial role of technology in navigating supply chain disruptions. We invested in sophisticated inventory management software that provided real-time tracking of medication levels, allowing us to anticipate shortages and proactively adjust our ordering strategies. This technology also enhanced communication with suppliers and patients, enabling us to inform patients promptly about potential delays or medication substitutions.

Real-time data and improved communication helped us maintain transparency and build stronger relationships with our patients, fostering trust and confidence during a turbulent period. The digital transformation not only streamlined our operations but also enhanced our overall effectiveness, ensuring we could respond to challenges swiftly and efficiently.

The challenges posed by shortages and supply chain disruptions underscore the need for enhanced collaboration across the healthcare system. We strengthened our relationships with our hospital colleagues, sharing information about medication availability and coordinating patient care.

This facilitated a more efficient allocation of resources across the healthcare system, maximizing the effectiveness of limited supplies. The collaborative approach reinforced the interdependence of healthcare providers and highlighted the importance of a cohesive, integrated system. This ongoing collaboration extended beyond the immediate crisis, shaping our approach to future challenges. We understood that preparedness and communication were paramount in addressing the inevitable complexities of our healthcare system.

Finally, our experience navigating the pandemic's supply chain crisis reinforced the vital importance of investing in domestic manufacturing and strengthening the resilience of our healthcare infrastructure. The pandemic exposed the vulnerabilities inherent in relying heavily on global supply chains, highlighting the urgent need for greater self-sufficiency in the production of essential medicines and medical supplies. This realization shaped our advocacy efforts, driving us to engage in discussions with policymakers and industry leaders to promote policies that support domestic manufacturing and enhance supply chain security. This advocacy demonstrated that the pharmacist's role extends beyond patient care, including impacting regulatory and legislative efforts to improve healthcare system resilience.

The pandemic's impact extended far beyond the immediate health crisis; it also created a perfect storm of financial and operational challenges for our charitable pharmacy. Our already tight budget was stretched to its breaking point by the increased demand for medications, the rising costs of acquiring scarce supplies, and the need for additional staff to manage the overwhelming workload.

The initial surge in COVID-19 cases brought a sudden and dramatic increase in demand for our services. Many individuals, newly unemployed or facing reduced work hours, found themselves unable to afford their medications.

Others, understandably anxious about their health and the future, turned to us for support and reassurance. This surge in demand, coupled with supply chain disruptions, amplified the pressure on our limited resources.

The cost of essential medications skyrocketed. We observed a significant increase in the wholesale prices of many drugs, particularly those in high demand for COVID-19 treatment.

This, combined with the difficulties in procuring supplies, forced us to make tough financial decisions. We had to carefully evaluate our spending, prioritize essential purchases, and explore creative solutions to stretch our limited resources. We initiated an emergency fundraising campaign, reaching out to our existing donors and seeking support from new community partners. We were heartened by the outpouring of generosity; individuals, local businesses, and even foundations stepped up to provide crucial financial support. This fundraising proved essential in maintaining our operations and ensuring we could continue to serve our community during a time of immense need.

However, fundraising alone wasn't enough. We needed to implement cost-cutting measures while simultaneously enhancing efficiency. We rigorously analyzed our operational expenses, identifying areas where we could reduce costs without compromising patient care. This included negotiating better prices with our suppliers, streamlining our administrative processes, and exploring cost-effective alternatives for packaging and delivery. We switched to more cost-effective packaging options, and we implemented a more efficient delivery system that reduced fuel costs. We also looked at consolidating our routes and utilizing volunteer drivers where possible. This careful planning and efficient allocation of resources allowed us to maximize the impact of every dollar we received, ensuring that our limited budget was used as effectively as possible.

Beyond the financial challenges, the pandemic also presented operational hurdles. Maintaining social distancing guidelines, ensuring staff and patient safety, and implementing new infection control protocols proved to be significant logistical undertakings. We quickly adapted our operations, implementing curbside pickup and drive-through medication dispensing. This ensured patients could access medications without compromising their safety. We invested in virtual telehealth technologies to communicate with patients remotely, providing medication counseling and answering questions about their treatment. The initial investment felt significant, but it was quickly recouped in the efficiency gains and the increased patient access.

We also had to address the increased risk of exposure for our staff. The pandemic brought unprecedented levels of stress and anxiety, not only for our patients but also for our team.

We initiated robust mental health support programs for our staff, providing access to counseling services and stress management workshops. Recognizing that our team's well-being was crucial to maintaining our operations, we prioritized their mental and physical health. We arranged for regular testing, provided personal protective equipment, and staggered work schedules to reduce potential exposures.

This proactive approach not only helped protect our staff but also helped maintain a high level of morale and team cohesion, both of which were crucial for sustaining our efforts.

Sustaining operations amidst such uncertainty also necessitated a high degree of flexibility and adaptability. We had to respond rapidly to changing circumstances, adjusting our policies and procedures as needed. The evolving guidelines from public health authorities demanded constant vigilance and prompt implementation of new safety measures. This required quick thinking, seamless communication, and a willingness to embrace innovative solutions. The constant adaptation was challenging but critical; we learned to anticipate changes and adapt rapidly, ensuring our continued operations. This constant adjustment required strong leadership and team cohesion, emphasizing the value of a well-trained and versatile staff capable of handling multiple demands.

One of the most significant challenges we faced was maintaining our commitment to equitable access to medications, especially for vulnerable populations. The pandemic disproportionately affected low-income communities and individuals with pre-existing conditions. Many of our patients, already struggling to make ends meet, found themselves in an even more precarious situation. We redoubled our efforts to provide assistance to these vulnerable populations, developing targeted outreach programs to ensure they continued to receive the medications they needed. We partnered with local social service organizations, community clinics, and food banks to identify and assist patients who were struggling to afford their prescriptions. This collaborative approach ensured that we were reaching those who needed our support the most.

We developed a streamlined system to prioritize prescriptions, ensuring that life-sustaining medications were dispensed quickly and efficiently. We also established a system for verifying patient insurance coverage and providing financial assistance when necessary. This involved working with various insurance companies, navigating complex regulations, and providing compassionate support to patients who were struggling. The process demanded a delicate balance of maintaining efficiency and ensuring that no patient was overlooked.

This experience underscored the importance of building strong relationships with our community partners. Our collaboration with local organizations extended far beyond the usual interactions; it became a lifeline during the crisis. We shared resources, information, and expertise, creating a powerful network of support. This collaboration not only ensured continuity of care for our patients but also strengthened the fabric of our community. It was a testament to the resilience and mutual support that can emerge in times of crisis. The partnerships forged during the pandemic proved invaluable and continue to shape our approach to community service.

The emotional toll of working under such extreme pressure cannot be overstated. Our staff faced extraordinary challenges, often working long hours under stressful conditions. They were not only responsible for dispensing medications but also for providing emotional support to anxious patients. They served as a calming presence, offering reassurance and hope during a time of great uncertainty.

Their commitment to serving our community, despite the personal sacrifices they made, was truly inspiring. We actively recognized and celebrated their efforts, ensuring they felt supported and appreciated.

From Bad to Worse

During flu season, everything we were already dealing with got worse. I remember one particularly intense week when demand for flu medications and other cold remedies surged. Patients lined up for hours, their faces masked by anxiety and worry. We did what we could, like answering questions and trying to keep things moving, but the stress was everywhere, on both sides of the counter. The staff worked nonstop, doing our best to keep up. Still, that week made something painfully clear: our community's access to care was fragile, and when a crisis hit, it cracked wide open. The gaps were obvious; those with limited access suffered disproportionately during peak health crises.

The emotional toll was immense. I kept thinking about the people who didn't have any coverage; what happened to them when they got sick? What happens to those who can barely afford essential medications? Witnessing the daily struggle of my patients left an indelible mark on my soul. "Back when Asha and I practiced together, we used to drop prices of medications low enough that people would be able to take them home. We cut our profit margin to almost nothing. It felt like a small victory amidst overwhelming challenges. But why did it have to be this way? Why was the system so broken, and why were so many people still left behind? The exhaustion, the frustration, the sense of helplessness—it all contributed to a profound sense of weariness. I found myself working longer hours, always feeling as if I wasn't doing enough, always feeling the pressure to offer more support, more understanding, more compassion than the system allowed. The emotional weight of these daily experiences took its toll.

This wasn't just about dispensing pills; it was about witnessing human suffering on a daily basis. My pharmacy in Keansburg served a community where many lived below the poverty line and often relied on local churches just to cover the cost of their meds, so it was about recognizing the deep and systemic inequalities that prevented people from accessing the healthcare they deserved. I saw that gap every day. And I realized being a pharmacist had to mean more than standing behind the counter. Asha and I talked about it all the time: how heavy it felt, how unfair it was. My amazing wife knew that if someone came into the pharmacy with a crisis, I would give the medications away as charity and write it off. That heart was always there. Maybe God created me this way, and Asha always stood by me in that. But even with Asha's unwavering support, it didn't make the weight any easier to carry.

It felt less like a job and more like a calling. I couldn't look away from the suffering in front of me and pretend someone else would deal with it. The experience was a powerful catalyst, shaping my future direction and cementing my conviction to establish a charitable pharmacy – a sanctuary of healthcare access for those most in need. It was a culmination of the emotional weight, the daily struggles witnessed in my patients, and the unyielding belief that something had to change, that better, more equitable access to healthcare had to be the norm, not the exception. Still, if I'm being honest, I didn't act right away. I didn't have the strength yet. Running five pharmacies and balancing other business obligations meant that the heart I had for service kept getting buried under everything else. I knew deep down something had to change. But responsibility kept pulling me in the opposite direction.

The weight of those experiences, the cumulative effect of witnessing daily struggles, finally crystallized into a concrete idea for the future of a charitable pharmacy. The concept wasn't a sudden epiphany, but rather a slow burn, a gradual coalescence of frustration, compassion, and unwavering determination. It came from those quiet conversations with patients who were scared about money, from the nights I couldn't sleep, from the growing conviction that this wasn't how healthcare was supposed to work. I kept thinking about the people who had nothing. The ones who got worse, not because their illness was untreatable, but because they couldn't afford treatment at all. As CEO of Legacy Pharmacy Group, I had the honor of working with over a thousand pharmacies during the pandemic. We all saw what that invisible enemy could do. Lives disappeared overnight. And then Rena passed in October 2021, and it hit even harder. What happens to the people who never even had a chance to fight back because they didn't have access to basic meds?

This reminds me of a conversation I once had with my little sister. Rena had called me saying that what I am doing for others and helping them brings lots of good *Punya* (good fortune), but do the same for *Garibs* – the poor. Her words lingered, echoing in my mind with a gravity that was impossible to ignore.

The initial seeds of the idea were sown not in a grand, dramatic moment, but in the quiet spaces between dispensing medications. It was during those moments, amidst the hum of the pharmacy, the rustling of prescription bags, and the quiet murmurs of patients, that the vision began to take shape. The image of a pharmacy free from the constraints of profit, a place where access to essential medications wasn't contingent upon financial stability, became a driving force.

The first step was a painstaking process of self-reflection and research. I spent countless hours poring over reports on healthcare disparities, studying the models of successful charitable organizations, and in November, I became a member of Charitable Pharmacies of America. Through that network, I connected with Toni and Donney John, who became important guides. I wanted to create something that would serve the underserved in a meaningful way, something that would honor Rena's memory. The challenge was daunting, but the urgency of the need fueled my resolve. I began by compiling detailed statistics on the prevalence of medication insecurity in my community, drawing on data from local health clinics like Parker, social service agencies, and my own pharmacy's records. The numbers were startling, a sobering reminder of the hidden struggles faced by many. These figures revealed the stark reality of the situation, highlighting the disproportionate burden borne by low-income families, the elderly, and individuals with chronic illnesses. Several in-depth conversations with the late Dr. Steve Honingman were very helpful as well. Dr. Honingman had spent decades advocating for equitable healthcare, and his insights were invaluable in shaping the structure of my initiative.

Simultaneously, I initiated preliminary discussions with potential collaborators. Reaching out to local community leaders, healthcare professionals, and non-profit organizations proved crucial. These initial conversations, though tentative, were surprisingly encouraging. Many shared similar concerns and expressed a desire to work together towards a common goal. These weren't just surface-level meetings, they turned into real collaborations. We sat around tables, shared frustrations, mapped out dreams, and figured out what might actually be possible. Every conversation made it feel a little more real, a little more urgent. It reminded me this wasn't just my fight; it belonged to all of us.

Starting the charitable pharmacy was one of the hardest things I've ever done. I had no roadmap; just a strong belief in the cause, a deep sense of responsibility, and the faces of my patients who needed better access to medicine. The early days were a blur of research, planning, and long nights. I studied legal requirements, drafted a business plan, looked into funding options, and tried to understand how to actually get medications into the hands of people who needed them. Every task was more difficult than expected, and the pressure often felt unbearable. Still, I kept going, driven by the need I saw every day and the support of the few people who believed in the vision with me.

Funding was the first major obstacle. I wrote grant after grant, pouring hours into proposals that were often met with silence or rejection. Each "no" stung, but I took every piece of feedback seriously. I rewrote, reworked, and learned how to tell the story of what we were trying to build in a way that connected with people. I also reached out beyond grants, talking to foundations, companies, and individuals, trying to build real partnerships, not just asking for money. It meant showing that we were serious, that we could be trusted, and that we had a plan. These conversations weren't easy. They took time, honesty, and patience.

Getting the medications themselves was another uphill battle. I had to convince pharmaceutical companies, wholesalers, and suppliers to work with us—a tiny, unproven nonprofit. Many were hesitant at first. They wanted to know if we could manage inventory properly, follow strict rules, and stay above board. I had to build trust, explain our mission clearly, and prove we weren't just another group with good intentions but no follow-through. Slowly, piece by piece, we built those relationships.

The legal side was no easier. Setting up a non-profit pharmacy meant dealing with layers of rules at the local, state, and federal level. We had to be precise with paperwork, careful with every decision, and ready to spend money on legal help when we didn't have much to spare. It wasn't glamorous work; it was hours spent on phone calls, forms, and compliance checklists, but it was necessary to build something that would last.

Emotionally, it took everything I had. I went from being a pharmacist with a steady job to someone carrying the weight of an entire project. There were nights I couldn't sleep, too anxious about what might fall through. I questioned myself constantly. Was this too big? Was I in over my head? But every small win, a grant approval, a donation, a partnership, helped pull me back up. We celebrated every step forward because we knew how hard each one was to earn.

None of it would have been possible alone. Building this pharmacy meant building a community. We found allies in hospitals, clinics, nonprofits, and community leaders. These weren't just connections, they were people who shared our purpose. Together, we built a network that helped patients get the care they needed and kept the project moving forward. We weren't just filling prescriptions; we were changing the way healthcare reached those who had been overlooked.

Looking back, it was never just about the logistics or the paperwork. It was about people. About showing up, even when it was hard. About staying honest, staying focused, and remembering why we started. The journey was long, full of setbacks, and tested every part of me. But in the end, we built something real, something rooted in compassion, trust, and the belief that healthcare shouldn't be a privilege. Every lesson, every challenge, every quiet moment of doubt added to the story. And the story wasn't just mine, it belonged to everyone who stood beside me, believed in the vision, and helped turn it into something that could truly make a difference.

Chief O'Hare and His Trip to Florida – A Small Family Cruise and Testing Almost 40 People in One Hour

One of the most memorable moments during the pandemic was helping my good friend, Chief O'Hare, and his extended family prepare for a long-awaited cruise to Florida. Chief O'Hare, a respected leader in our community, had lost several family members to COVID-19, and, understandably, his family was anxious about traveling. They were initially skeptical about the necessity of COVID testing, but their trust in me—as both a pharmacist and a friend—was strong. Chief O'Hare told his family he would only go through with the testing if I said it was the right thing to do.

With nearly 40 family members and friends needing to be tested within a tight window so they could safely board their cruise, we transformed his garage into a makeshift testing clinic.

My colleague Marissa Malstrom was by my side, helping organize the process, collect samples, and keep everyone calm and comfortable. The logistics were not easy- coordinating so many people, ensuring proper documentation, and providing reassurance to those who were nervous or hesitant. But together, we managed to test everyone efficiently, making sure each person felt cared for and respected.

For many in the group, this was their first time being tested, and their anxiety was palpable. But as the results started coming in–all negative–the mood shifted from tension to joy. Chief O'Hare and his family could finally exhale, knowing they could travel together and enjoy precious time on the cruise without the shadow of COVID hanging over them. The relief and happiness on their faces were the greatest reward I could ask for.

What made this experience especially meaningful was the trust Chief O'Hare placed in me. Despite his initial doubts about testing, his faith in my judgment allowed him and his family to move forward with confidence and peace of mind. Seeing them board that cruise, ready to make new memories after so much loss, filled me with a deep sense of purpose and gratitude.

That day in the garage was about more than just COVID tests- it was about restoring hope, protecting loved ones, and helping a family reclaim joy during uncertain times. Thanks to teamwork, compassion, and the trust of a friend, we turned a moment of anxiety into a celebration of life and togetherness.

Even after becoming CEO of Legacy Pharmacy Group— overseeing hundreds of independent pharmacies and leading major initiatives—I still get regular calls from Chief O'Hare asking for help as a pharmacist. I've told him many times that I'm not a "regular" pharmacist anymore, but Chief won't listen. To him, I'll always be his trusted healthcare advisor and friend.

Whether it's a question about medication, a concern about a family member's health, or just a need for reassurance, he reaches out to me without hesitation. And on the rare occasion he doesn't call, I find myself texting him early in the morning to check in— since we're both early risers.

Helping Chief over the years has created a deep bond between us—one that goes beyond professional courtesy. He's become like a big brother to me, and I affectionately call him my Irish brother. There's a unique joy and soul-satisfaction that comes from knowing our friendship was built on trust, care, and a shared commitment to family and community.

When Chief learned about my decision to open the Ritesh Shah Charitable Pharmacy, he didn't hesitate to join our mission. He now serves as a valued member of our advisory board, offering wisdom, leadership, and community insight to help us reach even more people in need. Having Chief by my side—as a friend and as a partner in service—is one of the greatest rewards of my journey as a pharmacist and leader.

Love you, Chief O'Hare—your faith in me continues to inspire my purpose every day.

Chapter 4: Before the Sun Rose: Silent Battles of a Pharmacist's Heart

The world will always remember the pandemic for its fear, its isolation, and its losses. But for those of us in pharmacy, those of us who served on the quiet front lines, it will forever be remembered differently. It was a time when our purpose woke before dawn, long before the sun lit the sky.

From the garage of our home, my wife Asha and I — two pharmacists bound not only by marriage but by mission — began collecting COVID specimens at unthinkable hours. It wasn't about the tests or the protocols. It was about the people: the essential workers who needed to do their jobs, the grieving families desperate to travel and say goodbye to a loved one, the everyday souls seeking a sliver of hope in the darkness. We opened pharmacy doors at 5 a.m., 6 a.m., whatever it took. When the world was afraid to move, we moved toward it, led only by duty and heart.

We fought silent battles daily. From long nights coordinating resources to early mornings loading supplies in the garage, every effort felt urgent—because it was. With testing sites overwhelmed and communities desperate for answers, we did everything possible to secure rapid tests and deliver them to those in need.

But even in the chaos, something sacred emerged. Every test collected, every worried face reassured—it was more than a clinical task. It was Seva. It was compassion in motion. It was the realization that our true power as pharmacists wasn't just in dispensing medication, but in standing as pillars of trust, presence, and hope during times of crisis.

Together with giants like Steve Honigman and Senator Vin Gopal, we fought to make sure pharmacists were seen for who they are: highly trained, deeply compassionate warriors in the battle for life itself. We advocated, we innovated, and we served — not because we had to, but because we were called.

Ours was a silent war, but a sacred oath. Healing a broken world, one act of compassion at a time.

This is what it truly means to be a pharmacist.

I will never forget those endless days — and nights — spent at the Freehold Borough Fire Station and local train stations, standing shoulder to shoulder with my fellow pharmacists and first responders. Nearly every day, including weekends, we were there, conducting COVID specimen collections in freezing weather, sometimes for hours on end. We worked closely with countless police departments, fire departments, and EMT teams, making sure they were tested, protected, and ready to return to duty. It wasn't just about their health; it was about the health of entire communities that depended on them. In those moments, it became clear: this was more than testing. It was a chain of service, a circle of protection, a sacred effort to keep hope alive — one precious human life at a time.

I will never forget those days — working closely with my small network of pharmacies, loading my personal car with COVID testing supplies, nebulizers, hand sanitizers, masks, even clothes, and driving from school to school. Freehold Borough, Red Bank Regional High School — wherever there was a need, we went. I remember dropping off a nebulizer at Freehold Borough, delivering hand sanitizers by the gallon, anything to protect the students, the teachers, the staff. It wasn't just about supplies; it was about standing in the gap between fear and safety, between sickness and hope. Those two lost years, from 2020 through 2021, became a defining time of purpose. Each delivery, each donation was an act of silent Seva — a way to honor life itself in a world that had lost so much.

During those early, chaotic months of the pandemic, when basic protective supplies were nearly impossible to find, we knew we had to do more than wait. We began partnering with agencies across the country and even overseas to import life-saving supplies. Masks, gloves, sanitizers, gowns, the simple things that had suddenly become as precious as gold. It was not about business. It was not about profit. It was about survival. It was about humanity.

We worked around the clock to source and secure these critical supplies, not only for our pharmacies but for local schools, community centers, houses of worship, and even hospitals that were overwhelmed and desperate. I still remember doctors and highly respected physicians coming directly to my home, knocking on my door, to pick up whatever we could spare so they could continue caring for their patients. These were not transactions. They were sacred exchanges, from one heart to another, from one healer to another.

We weren't trying to build a business empire. We were trying to build a lifeline. In a world that was losing millions of human lives, every mask, every gown, every box of gloves we secured felt like sending out a lifeboat into a drowning sea.

We simply asked ourselves one question every single day: "How many more lives can we save today?"

During those times, it was never about my physical body — the exhaustion, the cold, the endless hours. It wasn't about me at all. It was about the pharmacist within me, the calling inside me that spoke louder than any fatigue. Every single day, that inner voice reminded me: "Help your neighbors. Help your patients. Help your community." It became my compass. It became my oxygen. Even when the world stood still in fear, I kept moving — not because I had to, but because my heart as a pharmacist left me no choice. Service became my survival. Purpose became my pulse.

But even with all the service, all the sleepless nights, and all the lives we tried so hard to protect, life still had its own painful plans. In October of 2021, I traveled to India — a journey that would forever mark my soul. It was there, amidst a country still healing from the devastation of the pandemic, that I faced the most personal loss of all.

My baby sister, Rena, who had battled her own underlying conditions, including diabetes, heart disease, and mental health struggles, became one more precious soul stolen by this unseen, unstoppable virus. The ache of losing her was like no other pain I had ever known. It was not just the loss of a sister; it was the loss of dreams, laughter, and childhood memories. It was the silent scream of every patient I had ever tried to save, now crashing into my own home.

I cried. I cried. I cried. I was shattered.

Standing in the place where she once smiled, I realized something deeper than grief. I realized the profound power of love and memory.

All the years of service, all the nights of sacrifice, and all the acts of Seva had shaped me for this very calling.

Rena's life, her struggles, and her gentle spirit became the seed of a greater purpose. From her memory was born a mission that would carry her light forward — to create a charitable pharmacy that would stand as a living testament to compassion, dignity, and service. A place where no patient would be left behind because they couldn't afford their medicine.

Her loss didn't break me. It built me.

It built the purpose I was always meant to fulfill.

The trip to India in October 2021 was meant to be a celebration, a homecoming of the heart. After almost twenty-five years away, I was finally returning to celebrate Diwali, the festival of lights, with my beloved sister Rena. Even more special was the day after Diwali, Bhai Bij, a sacred day in India when brothers and sisters honor their bond.

It was a perfect plan.

Rena was preparing to immigrate to the United States in 2022. We were ready to reunite and build new memories together on the soil of our shared dreams. I could feel her excitement and her pure joy. For both of us, this was more than a festival. It was the beginning of a new chapter.

But God had different plans.

Rena often told me in her simple and profound way, "God has been good to you. You should do something for those who don't have anything." She had such a tender heart, shaped by her own battles. She once said to me, "You are a pharmacist. Giving medications to poor people is a blessing too." I didn't realize then how her words would one day echo so loudly in my soul.

Losing her during the pandemic was the hardest blow I had ever endured. But somehow, even in the midst of unbearable grief, her spirit lit a candle inside me that has never gone out. She became the voice inside my heart, whispering, guiding, and reminding me that my true purpose was never just to dispense pills.

It was to dispense hope.

It was to serve those who had been forgotten.

And so, from the ashes of loss, the seed of the Ritesh Shah Charitable Pharmacy was planted — a living tribute to Rena's life, her dreams, and her endless belief in compassion.

Rena didn't leave us empty.

She left behind two beautiful children — her niece and nephew — and an amazing brother-in-law who has now made their home in Texas. Both of her children, with hearts full of determination and dreams full of purpose, are on their way to becoming pharmacists. It feels like her spirit is living on through them, continuing the work she always believed in.

During Rena's prayer ceremony in Himmatnagar, India, as Asha and I sat there surrounded by family, memories, and immeasurable grief, a quiet but powerful decision was made in our hearts. We realized that when we returned home to Freehold, we couldn't simply go back to life as it was. We needed to create something lasting. Something bigger than our pain. Something that would turn her memory into a movement.

That was the moment the vision of the charitable pharmacy truly took root.

Not just another pharmacy, but a powerful symbol of what Rena Shah stood for: kindness, service, compassion, and hope.

We made a silent promise that her name, her spirit, and her legacy would live on. They would be forever woven into the logo, the mission, and the very soul of the Ritesh Shah Charitable Pharmacy.

So many captions came to mind:

"When you serve with love, no one you lose is ever truly gone."

"Through every prescription filled, every life touched, her spirit lives on."

"In giving hope to others, I keep her light burning forever."

"A sister's love became my life's greatest purpose."

Her story did not end.

It transformed into a thousand acts of kindness.

Grief carved an empty space inside me, but purpose poured in to fill it. Every life we touch, every medicine we give, every hand we hold is a promise kept. A sister's wish turned into a mission far greater than I ever imagined.

She taught me, in her own quiet way, that true wealth was never in what we owned, but in how much we gave. Today, the Ritesh Shah Charitable Pharmacy is not just a building. It is the living heartbeat of her kindness, echoing through every soul we serve.

When I returned home from India carrying the heavy weight of losing my beloved sister, I knew I could not let her story end there.

Rena's voice, her dreams, her wishes — they echoed inside me louder than ever.

In the midst of grief, I found a mission. A calling to serve the underserved, to heal the forgotten, and to light the way for those who had no other hope.

The Ritesh Shah Charitable Pharmacy was born not just out of sorrow, but out of a brother's promise to keep his sister's light.

Some moments in life change everything forever.

Losing Rena during the pandemic shattered my heart, but it also revealed a new path — a life of deeper meaning, of true service, of turning loss into legacy.

With my wife Asha by my side and my deep belief in Seva, or selfless service, to guide me, I made a silent promise. I would build something lasting. Something that would honor Rena's spirit through every life we touched.

That is how the Ritesh Shah Charitable Pharmacy was born — not from sorrow alone, but from love, hope, and a brother's eternal promise to keep his sister's light shining.

In the quiet moments after Rena's prayer ceremonies, Asha and

I talked about what it would mean to truly honor her spirit.

We knew it had to be more than just words or memories.

Back home in Freehold, New Jersey, that vision began to take shape. We imagined a pharmacy where no one would be turned away because of money. A place where dignity and compassion would fill every prescription. A place where the forgotten would be remembered, the underserved would be seen, and the uninsured would be treated with the same care as anyone else.

But dreams are only the beginning. The journey to build the Ritesh Shah Charitable Pharmacy was filled with challenges— from finding a location, navigating endless paperwork, understanding regulations, and assembling a team that believed in the same mission. There were moments of doubt, of frustration, of exhaustion.

Yet every step, every obstacle, every late-night worry felt lighter when I remembered why we were doing it.

Rena's light guided us. Her blessings pushed us forward. Every time a door closed, a window opened, as if the universe itself wanted this mission to happen. And slowly, with grace and grit, the pharmacy was born — not just as a building, but as a beacon of hope for so many who had been left behind.

In the middle of so much pain and grief, when the idea of the Ritesh Shah Charitable Pharmacy was just taking shape, it wasn't a decision I made alone.

We had a family discussion — one of the most meaningful conversations of my life. Sitting together with Sarthak, Krina, and Arsha, we talked not just about logistics, but about love, about legacy, and about the purpose we wanted to live for.

I will never forget what Asha, my wife, said that day. After 25 years of marriage, she looked at me with her signature kindness and said with a smile,

"I will be nice to you again — and I will put my white coat back on. I will go back to work as a volunteer, so we can serve together and keep Rena's light alive."

In that moment, I realized: this was not just my mission. It was our family's mission. Together, we would turn our grief into giving, our loss into love, and our pain into a purpose that would touch countless lives.

Pills to Purpose is not just my story.

Pills to Purpose is our story — mine and Asha's.

Without Asha, the Purpose would have remained just an idea in my heart. It was her strength, her belief, her quiet sacrifices that helped turn a dream into a living, breathing mission.

In every challenge, she stood with me. In every moment of doubt, she reminded me why we started. In every act of service, she brought her compassion and her white coat back into the world — not for recognition, but for love.

This is our story of love, of loss, of resilience, and of a promise kept.

Pills to Purpose is the story of how two pharmacists, two souls, came together to transform grief into hope and how, through every life we touch, Rena's light continues to shine.

This mission, this book, is dedicated to Rena, whose light continues to guide us.

It is also dedicated to my wife, Asha, without whom this journey would have never been possible.

As two pharmacists, working side by side for more than 20 years, we have witnessed the silent struggles — the healthcare disparities, the patients who slipped through the cracks, the families who suffered simply because they could not afford the medications they needed to survive.

Together, we have shared a belief that access to care is not a privilege; it is a human right.

Pills to Purpose is our way of standing up for that belief.

It is a living promise that no one should ever be forgotten. That even in loss, there is a way to heal. When two hearts come together with love and service, miracles are possible.

This is for Rena.

This is for every patient we've ever served.

This is for everyone who believes that giving is the purest form of healing.

Chapter 5: The White Coat Beside Me – Asha's Journey of Selfless Support

There are many kinds of strength in this world. Some shout loudly from the stage. Others move quietly in the background, holding everything together. Asha is the second kind. The kind of person whose steady hands and calm heart have been the foundation of my life, my family, and our entire journey through pharmacy.

We've always worked side by side, not just as business partners, but as life partners. Through every pharmacy launch, every setback, every milestone, and every long night sorting out inventory or managing prescriptions, Asha has been there—focused, present, unwavering. From the beginning, she gave her all because she believed in the vision we were building. She believed in me, even when I didn't.

After graduating from St. John's Pharmacy College in New York, she entered the pharmacy world with quiet determination. She began her career at Drug Emporium in the late '90s, then went on to work at Rite Aid, Walmart, and independent pharmacies. What made her unique wasn't just her professionalism, but the way she used her off days—not for rest, but to build the future we dreamed of. In 2002, she gave up her dream car and saved every dollar so that we could open Bayshore Homecare Pharmacy in Holmdel. That kind of sacrifice can't be taught. It has to come from the heart.

By the time we opened Ramtown Pharmacy in 2005, Asha was the one holding everything up. She served as pharmacist-in-charge while also returning home to care for our children. She handled both roles with grace. Our kids' education was never compromised, and the pharmacy never missed a prescription. She gave her all, quietly, behind the curtain. It wasn't just the act of multitasking that made her role extraordinary; it was the unwavering consistency with which she showed up, every single day. Whether it was a child's school event or a drug order that needed to be double-checked, Asha was always the one who had it under control. There were nights she stayed up with the kids to help them study, only to wake up early and head to the pharmacy. She brought the same dedication to her family as she did to her patients, making sure no one ever felt neglected, not at home, not at work, not in our hearts.

As our business grew, we expanded to Martinsville, Raritan, Keansburg, Matawan, and Red Bank. Each step forward had her fingerprints on it. Even when she wasn't physically present in every store, her presence was felt. Her insights, her careful planning, and the way she helped me avoid costly mistakes were what made those expansions possible. While I might have been the one out in the community, talking to doctors, attending meetings, or speaking at events, it was Asha who made sure the foundation never cracked beneath us.

She didn't do it for praise or recognition. In fact, she would always deflect any kind of attention directed her way. But the truth is, those pharmacies wouldn't have been sustainable without her quiet leadership and unwavering focus. Every system that ran smoothly, every team member who felt supported, every patient who received their medication on time—Asha's touch was in all of it.

"Success is best when it's shared." That quote lives in Asha's actions more than her words. She never asked for applause, but every bit of success we've achieved is a shared journey because of the way she walked beside me through every high and low.

Asha has always had the kind of listening skills most people only wish for. I could speak for hours, sharing my frustrations, my hopes, my ideas, and she would sit quietly, fully present, taking it all in. She never interrupted, never looked distracted, and never made me feel like I was taking up too much space. Even when her own day had been long and full, she created space for me to unload mine. Her ability to listen without rushing, to simply be there with me in the moment, gave me the sense that everything could be figured out. That kind of patience and calm was rare, and it always gave me a sense of peace.

When she did respond, her words were few but powerful. She never needed to say much. Her thoughts were always clear and honest, often cutting through all the noise in my head. It was as if she could hold the mess of my thinking gently in her hands and give it back to me in a more settled form. It was during those quiet conversations that I truly understood how lucky I was to have her by my side. Asha didn't just hear me; she understood me. And in that understanding, she gave me the confidence to face whatever was coming next.

When I received my first "Pharmacist of the Year" award in 2010, the pride in her eyes was unforgettable. It was as if the award had been given to both of us, because in every sense, it truly had. That moment reflected not just my efforts, but the late nights, the sacrifices, the encouragement, and the steady hand Asha had always provided behind the scenes. She never asked for the spotlight, never needed her name on the plaque, but her presence was woven into every success I had.

She stood beside me at every moment that led to that recognition—through the tough decisions, the setbacks, and the little wins we often celebrated quietly over tea at home. Even when things were going well, Asha kept me grounded. She reminded me of why we started and who we were doing it all for. And when things fell apart, when the stress became overwhelming or when plans didn't go as expected, she was the one who held us together. Her calm was the glue that kept everything from breaking.

As Mahatma Gandhi once said, "Strength does not come from physical capacity. It comes from an indomitable will." Asha's quiet strength, her unwavering will, and her belief in our shared vision made all the difference.

One of the lowest points in our journey was losing our Raritan pharmacy. We lost nearly all our savings with it. I couldn't shake the failure. It felt personal. I was sinking fast. That's when Asha stepped in with the words that pulled me out. She said, "So what if we lost the pharmacy and the savings? If we have to go back to an apartment, we'll do that. But don't hurt yourself over this. I'm with you. We're both pharmacists. We'll get back on our feet." That strength, that simple belief, became my lifeline. She reminded me of who we were and what we were capable of, not just as businesspeople, but as a family.

Our life as pharmacists wasn't glamorous, but it had rhythm. Asha and I developed a routine that kept everything moving. She would head out early in the morning to open the pharmacy, and I would meet with doctors or work on marketing and outreach. By evening, we'd both be back home, switching gears from pharmacists to parents.

While I was juggling meetings, new partnerships, or community projects, Asha was quietly holding everything else together. She managed our home with the same precision and care she brought to her work. Dinner was always on time. The kids never missed their schoolwork or extracurriculars. The banking was handled, the bills were paid, and the pharmacy paperwork—everything from controlled substance logs to insurance audits—was perfectly in order. I often joke that our accountant, Dharmeshbhai, probably trusts Asha more than he trusts me. And there's some truth to that. Her consistency builds trust, whether at home or in business.

I've made my share of messes—literal and figurative—but she never complained. After every long day, she'd quietly clean up after me at the pharmacy, resetting things so the next morning started fresh. And somehow, even with the chaos of parenting, business, and everything in between, she made time for us. Each morning, over a cup of tea, we'd talk. Sometimes about work, sometimes about life, but always with honesty. Her advice in those quiet moments often shaped the decisions I made later in the day.

We argued, of course. Sometimes we clashed hard, especially when the stress got high. There were even days we wanted to strangle each other. But even in those moments, I knew that we'd figure it out. She was never out to win an argument; she wanted us to move forward. Every disagreement made me more self-aware. Every conversation helped me see something new in myself. That's the kind of partner she is: one who challenges you to grow without making you feel small.

People often ask me what Asha is like. I always say she's a tough cookie. Calm, cool, and composed, but with a fierce strength beneath the surface. She doesn't like the spotlight and never wants to be the center of attention. She'd rather be the one helping everything run smoothly behind the scenes. But make no mistake—she's the reason so much of it runs at all.

During the pandemic, when uncertainty gripped the world, we found ourselves on the front lines again. We worked side by side at the Union County vaccination clinic and later at the Freehold Fire Station. Every morning, Asha put on her white coat without hesitation. No complaints. No demands. Just a quiet commitment to help. She worked long hours with our team, making sure people were cared for, vaccinated, and reassured. She didn't ask for credit or compensation. She did it because that's who she is.

Her selflessness extended far beyond the pandemic. At the Ritesh Shah Charitable Pharmacy, she handled the paperwork, managed operations, and made sure everything ran efficiently. She even gave up the rental income from our property so we could dedicate the building to charity. That decision wasn't easy, especially with a family to support and financial pressures always lingering, but she never once hesitated. To her, helping people has always mattered more.

Asha has always balanced many roles, often without recognition. In our culture, women don't always get the credit they deserve. Yet she has stood tall, supporting her family here in the U.S. and back in India. Whether it was helping relatives navigate immigration paperwork, caring for elderly parents, or making sure our kids felt secure and loved, she never let anything fall through the cracks.

Her sacrifices have shaped our lives in ways that are hard to describe. She didn't just support my career—she built it alongside me. Every milestone I've reached, every honor I've received, has been possible because she made space for it to happen.

One of the most defining moments of our journey came in 2021, after the sudden and heartbreaking loss of my sister, Rena. That grief was unlike anything I had experienced. It left a hole that couldn't be filled with work or words. I was shattered. I needed something meaningful to hold onto—a way to honor her memory with purpose.

It was Asha who brought clarity during that fog. Without hesitation, she said that we should open a charitable pharmacy. I knew then that I hadn't just married a partner, I had married a visionary, someone who felt things deeply but always acted with strength. Opening the Ritesh Shah Charitable Pharmacy wasn't just a business decision; it was a deeply personal, spiritual calling. And Asha was with me every step of the way.

She handled the logistics, prepared the paperwork, met with our attorney, and coordinated with our accountant. While I dealt with the emotional toll, she dealt with the practical side, one steady step at a time. She made the mission hers. Even today, she shows up at the charitable pharmacy, wearing her white coat, greeting patients, and managing the daily details so that I can keep my head above water.

This wasn't something she did because she had extra time. Quite the opposite. She was still balancing the needs of our kids, our home, and multiple businesses. But her sense of duty—to family, to community, to legacy—has never wavered. If anything, it has grown stronger.

We talk a lot about leadership, about courage and compassion in healthcare. But few people embody all those qualities the way Asha does. Her leadership is quiet but powerful. Her courage is shown in the countless sacrifices she's made without ever making a show of them. Her compassion? You see it in the way she treats our staff, the way she listens to patients, the way she continues to serve even when she's tired or unwell.

At times, I've worried that she's given too much of herself. That she's poured so much into others—into me, our kids, our businesses, our community—that there might be nothing left for her. But she's never seen it that way. For her, this life we've built has always been a shared one. It's not about whose name is on the award, or who gives the speech. It's about making a difference, together.

And she has made all the difference.

Even our children have been deeply shaped by her example. They've seen what it means to work hard, to stay grounded, to help others. They've seen a mother who gave up sleep, comforts, and countless opportunities so they could flourish. It's no surprise that both of them are walking paths that serve others. The values they carry were learned from watching their mother lead—not with words, but with actions.

When I think about how far we've come, from saving up every dollar to start our first pharmacy to now running multiple businesses and a charitable organization, I know none of it would have happened without Asha. Not just because of her work ethic, but because of her values. She's never let us forget who we are or why we started. She keeps us honest, grounded, and focused. And above all, she is the reason I believe in partnership, not just in marriage or business, but in life. A partnership where love isn't always spoken, but always shown. Where support isn't conditional, but constant. Where two people walk side by side, lifting each other up, building something bigger than themselves.

Chapter 6: Service Beyond the Counter

As my pharmacies grew, so did my understanding that true health care cannot stop at the pharmacy door.

Being a pharmacist meant being an advocate, not just for the patients who walked into my stores but also for the communities that needed care and didn't know where to find it.

Early in my career, around 2003 or 2004, I joined the Indian Health Camp of New Jersey. At the time, I was simply looking for a way to give back. I had no idea that this partnership would evolve into one of the longest and most meaningful journeys of my life.

At health camps hosted in temples, community centers, and schools across the state, I volunteered my services as a pharmacist, offering counseling, providing free medications, answering questions, and helping to fill a gap where no one else was stepping in.

I will never forget the faces. The elderly woman who broke down in tears when we handed her adult diapers that she could never afford. The young man, newly diagnosed with diabetes, was overwhelmed and afraid, but left that day with both medication and hope.

Later, I would proudly serve as a member of the Board of Trustees for Indian Health Camp, working alongside incredible leaders like Dr. Tushar Patel and a deeply dedicated volunteer team.

My wife, Asha, who is also a pharmacist, often stood by my side during these camps. Together, we witnessed firsthand the health care disparities that left so many of our neighbors vulnerable and forgotten.

Over the past twenty years, volunteering has become a part of our family's DNA. Even our son, Sarthak, joined us to see what *Seva* truly meant. Seva, or selfless service, was not just a word—it was an action. It meant standing in Gandhi's footsteps and giving without asking for anything in return.

In addition to Indian Health Camp, I also gave my time to the Erskine Foundation, helping diabetic patients manage their conditions through education and support. I received awards and recognition along the way—honors like Pharmacist of the Year and various community leadership accolades—but it was never about plaques or certificates.

It was always about people. It was about the heart.

Every health camp, every donation, every counseling session became another stone laid on the road that would eventually lead to something greater than I could have imagined. A mission of service, built not only from professional success, but from love, loss, and purpose.

Building a Dream Out of Love

After returning from India in late 2021, my heart was heavy but focused. Losing Rena had changed me permanently. I had found my purpose: to serve those who had no access to the medications and care they desperately needed.

But how do you respect a soul that meant everything to you? How do you take the love, the pain, the emptiness — and turn it into something lasting?

For me, the answer was clear: I was going to open a charitable pharmacy.

In January 2022, Asha and I sat down with our family, Sarthak and Krina. We had long conversations, some emotional, some uncertain. Could we really do this? Could we give up rental income from our Shrewsbury Avenue building in Red Bank, a property that had been part of our family's financial security?

But when the question was framed as: Can we do this to honor Rena? There was no hesitation.

We decided: Yes.

The building would no longer be just a place of business. It would become a place of healing, a place of hope.

That decision set in motion one of the most intense, meaningful journeys of my life.

We had to create a 501(c)(3) nonprofit foundation.

We had to find attorneys who could help us build the right legal framework. We had to research models of charitable pharmacies across the country. We had to present to the New Jersey Board of Pharmacy, making the case for why New Jersey needed its first and only charitable pharmacy.

I cannot express how many hours went into meetings, documentation, vision presentations, and planning sessions.

But when you are trying to do God's work, miracles start happening.

People began to show up.

Not just any people — the right people.

Leaders, thinkers, healers. Each brought their unique talents and hearts to the table. We built an advisory board full of incredible souls — people who believed in the mission with the same fire that burned inside me.

It wasn't easy. Every step required faith. Every meeting demanded passion. Every roadblock tested our resolve.

But what we were building was bigger than all of us.

We were building a place where no patient would ever again have to choose between their next meal and their next dose of medicine.

We were building a place where Rena's light would never dim.

On the foundation of loss, pain, and love, we were laying the first stones of a new legacy:

The Ritesh Shah Charitable Pharmacy — New Jersey's First and Only Charitable Pharmacy.

Building a Mission from Heartbreak to Hope

After returning from India with a heavy heart and a renewed sense of purpose, Asha and I made a decision that would forever change not only our lives but also the lives of countless underserved patients. In January 2022, sitting with our family — Sarthak, Krina, and Arsha — we decided to turn our building at 224 Shrewsbury Avenue, Red Bank, into a sacred space: a charitable pharmacy dedicated to Rena's memory. It wasn't an easy decision. That building was my rental income, a steady stream that contributed to our family's livelihood. But when we weighed it against the opportunity to honor Rena's life and spirit, the choice became clear.

Purpose over profit. Seva over security.

From that point, every step was a testament to faith and perseverance. We built a strong foundation, both legally and spiritually. I gathered a brilliant group of advisors — pharmacists, physicians, healthcare executives, nonprofit experts, and community leaders — all who believed in this mission without hesitation. We completed numerous board presentations, built compliance systems, connected with community partners, and gathered data to illustrate the profound need.

We applied to the New Jersey Board of Pharmacy and, after careful planning and countless prayers, we were officially licensed, becoming New Jersey's first and only charitable pharmacy.

When you truly walk toward God's work, doors open.

He sent the right people at the right time: mentors, advisors, volunteers, and donors — all aligned with the vision. Our leadership team, highlighted on RSCP's website, became an extension of our family. Each member brought their unique expertise to help build an organization focused on reducing health disparities through free access to medications, immunizations, and patient education.

Our mission became crystal clear: to increase access to life-saving medications for uninsured and underserved patients. Our vision was simple but powerful: to create a healthier, more equitable community.

In these moments, I realized:

Everything — from my early pharmacy career starting at Bayshore Homecare Pharmacy in Holmdel, Ramtown Pharmacy in Howell, Drugsmart Pharmacy in Raritan, Martinsville Pharmacy, Drugsmart in Keansburg, Shrewsbury Avenue Pharmacy, to Marlboro Medical Arts Pharmacy — was not random. It was preparing me for this.

The Power of Relationships and Purpose

After years of dedicating myself to the profession — building successful pharmacies across New Jersey — I eventually stepped away from the day-to-day operations of these businesses to take on a broader leadership role. As CEO of Legacy Pharmacy Group, I shifted my focus to empowering independent pharmacies, creating opportunities, and strengthening the voice of pharmacists everywhere.

Little did I know, the network I had built — the relationships I had nurtured through years of honesty, hard work, and service — would become the very foundation of the mission ahead.

When the time came to open Ritesh Shah Charitable Pharmacy, these same colleagues, friends, and fellow healthcare warriors with big hearts didn't hesitate. They understood the spirit of the mission because they had witnessed my journey. They knew this wasn't just another project. This was the purpose.

So many stood beside us, bringing their expertise, their time, and their energy to the table. What we built wasn't just a charitable pharmacy; we built a community of hope, a family of Seva, grounded in two decades of trust and service.

When you live a life of genuine giving, the universe — and humanity — rise to meet you.

Opening the Doors: The First Days of Ritesh Shah Charitable Pharmacy

When we finally decided to move forward with the Ritesh Shah Charitable Pharmacy, it felt like standing at the edge of a new beginning. It was sacred, emotional, and full of purpose.

Behind the scenes, the journey was anything but easy. There were regulations to navigate, foundations to create, and an entirely new infrastructure to build. But every time I found myself weighed down by the uncertainty or the heavy responsibility, I had Senator Vin Gopal standing beside me.

During the pandemic, when the world was overwhelmed and confused, Vin stood beside us. With his help, we weren't just supporting families in Monmouth County, we were reaching people across the state, especially those who couldn't even get basic COVID testing. He helped make sure we were doing what was right, not just what was easy. And he never hesitated.

What most people don't know is that just two weeks before his second-term election, I flew to India to be with my family. That's when I lost my sister, Rena.

When I returned, I was shattered. But Vin didn't let me fall through the cracks. He called me almost every day, checking in, making sure I was okay, and reminding me why this work mattered. He didn't let the silence of grief swallow me whole. Instead, he helped me hold on to what Rena stood for. He reminded me that even though she was gone, her spirit could still move through me through service, through purpose, through the vision I had carried in my heart.

Vin never let me forget what I had set out to do. And in those conversations, I found the courage to keep going.

He helped me believe I could still bring this idea to life. And for that, I'll always be grateful.

His genuine care, along with the support of so many friends, advisors, and community leaders, gave me the strength to keep going. It showed me that when your mission is pure, the right people will walk with you through the darkest valleys toward the brightest light.

The day we began the formal steps to open New Jersey's first and only charitable pharmacy was not just a milestone.

It was the manifestation of Rena's love, my family's sacrifice, and a community's boundless belief that we can do better for one another — that no one should be without care because of their circumstances.

It was the beginning of a movement, not just a pharmacy.

Pills to Purpose – Continuing the Journey

Throughout my twenty years of serving as a pharmacist, I saw a reality that deeply troubled my heart — so many patients falling through the cracks, with no access to the life-saving medications they needed. I witnessed firsthand how bureaucracy, endless paperwork, and complicated systems often stood between a suffering patient and simple care. It hurt. Deep down, I knew that healthcare was a human right, not a privilege.

When I returned from India, after the painful loss of my beloved sister Rena, the calling inside me grew louder. It was no longer just about my successful pharmacy career — it was about answering a greater purpose. I made a silent promise to myself, to Rena, and to every patient who had ever walked into my pharmacies: I would open a door that would not turn anyone away.

Yes, the process was long. Yes, the regulations were heavy. But my spirit, and the spirit of my family standing with me, was stronger. We poured everything we had into founding the Ritesh Shah Charitable Pharmacy — New Jersey's first and only charitable pharmacy — not because it was easy, but because it was necessary.

I wasn't willing to let mountains of paperwork, insurance denials, or broken systems define the fate of my neighbors. Instead, I decided to be the bridge between despair and dignity, between sickness and healing, between hopelessness and hope.

When the doors of our Charitable Pharmacy finally opened, it wasn't just a building.

It was a promise fulfilled.

It was Rena's light shining.

It was my oath as a pharmacist — to serve, to heal, to love —

coming alive in the purest way.

This mission could not have been fulfilled alone. By my side, every step of the way, stood Asha — my wife, my partner, and my unwavering source of strength. A proud graduate of St.

John's University, and the daughter of a retired pharmacist, Asha's roots in pharmacy ran deep. But even deeper were her values: service, sacrifice, and an unconditional commitment to others.

When the idea of the charitable pharmacy was just a dream in my heart, Asha believed in it as fiercely as I did. She didn't just stand by; she put on her pharmacist's white coat once again — after years away from active practice — and volunteered every single day for over a year and six months. No salary, no complaints. Only purpose. Only love.

She served side-by-side with me, helping underserved patients walk out with life-saving medications and dignity, not despair. Her selflessness breathed life into every prescription filled, every heart touched, every story rewritten with hope.

Without her sacrifice and unconditional support, Pills to Purpose would have been a dream deferred. Today, she continues to serve, still fueled by the same fire of giving back, still keeping Rena's light — and our shared purpose — alive.

A Special Thank You to Asha

To my beloved wife, Asha — thank you for being the heart behind this mission. Your quiet strength, unwavering belief, and willingness to sacrifice everything for a greater cause gave Pills to Purpose its true soul. Watching you put your pharmacist's coat back on, volunteering day after day without hesitation, reminded me that love, when rooted in service, has no limits. This charitable pharmacy carries not just my sister's memory, but the selfless spirit you embody every single day.

Asha — The True Pillar Behind the Purpose

In the darkest hours after losing Rena, it was Asha who stood like a lighthouse in the storm. Every morning, as I went to work and she headed to the pharmacy to volunteer, she would wipe my tears and remind me, "She is smiling down upon us." Our pharmacy, to her, was not just a place to dispense medications — it was a temple, where we kept Rena's light alive with every act of kindness.

Asha, a proud graduate of St. John's University, a daughter and sister to pharmacists, chose to live her values through action. For one year and six months, she served every single day as a volunteer pharmacist, without expecting anything in return. To date, she handles day-to-day stuff behind the scenes and continues her Seva, so the purpose is on. It's a lot to sacrifice. Yet, in Asha's eyes, the sacrifice never felt like a burden. Her love, sacrifice, and quiet encouragement became the foundation of this charitable mission. Every morning, as Asha prepared to serve, her purpose glowed brightly, fueled by the memory of Rena and the spirit of giving. It was as though in every medication dispensed, she delivered a piece of hope, a fragment of care, a token of remembrance.

Without her — her hands holding mine, her faith strengthening my broken heart — Pills to Purpose would have remained just an idea. She gave it breath. She gave it life.

Letter from My Heart

Asha, you were my silent strength when I had none left. When the world felt heavy, when Rena's absence broke pieces of my soul, it was you who stood next to me, never letting me fall. Every day you chose to smile for me, even when your own heart was heavy. You whispered hope when all I could feel was loss. You built this dream of service with me — brick by brick, heart by heart.

This pharmacy is not only Rena's legacy. It's yours too. Thank you for believing in me, even when I could barely believe in myself.

Thank you for walking this sacred path with me, hand in hand, heart in heart.

This book is dedicated to the light that never fades — My beloved sister Rena, whose spirit and love inspired every step of this journey.

You are the heartbeat of this mission, the silent prayer behind every pill we dispense with purpose.

And to my wife, Asha — We had an arranged marriage, two pharmacists coming together by tradition.

But little did we know, God had already written a divine plan for us:

To walk this earth side by side, to heal, to serve, and to open New Jersey's first and only charitable pharmacy.

Our pair was made in heaven, not just for each other, but for a purpose greater than ourselves.

Asha, you are the soul of this story.

Your sacrifices, your strength, and your endless belief wiped away my tears when I had none left to give.

You stood beside me, smiling, believing, serving, so that together, we could keep Rena's light shining in this sacred temple we call Ritesh Shah Charitable Pharmacy.

To Rena, to Asha, and to the countless lives we are yet to touch — This is for you.

This is our Pills to Purpose.

Purpose is born when love meets loss, when healing meets hurt, and when two hands join not to hold each other, but to lift the world.

In every pill we give, in every life we touch, we are keeping her light alive.

Chapter 7: A Sister's Love: The Heart Behind My Mission

Growing up, my sister Rena was a simple, easygoing person. She wasn't seen as particularly smart, brave, or outgoing in the world's eyes, but to us, she was our only sister among three brothers—a quiet light in our lives. Our childhood was filled with laughter, shared secrets, and the kind of sibling love that doesn't always require deep conversations to feel real.

After we immigrated to the United States in 1997, our bond continued across the miles. We stayed connected through phone calls, brief visits, and small gestures—meals she lovingly cooked when I visited, thoughtful gifts she sent during Rakhi. Her unseen presence brought me comfort and joy. She had a way of making even the most ordinary moments feel special, and her laughter could brighten the darkest of days. She lived simply, but her love ran deep.

Lessons Learned from Her Strength and Spirit

One of my last visits to India was for my niece's wedding. Looking back, I am grateful I made time for that trip. At Asha's suggestion, I took a solo photo with Rena—and I thank God I did. It was a moment I now treasure deeply.

Despite facing her own health challenges, Rena never let her spirit falter. She lived with resilience, optimism, and a quiet strength that inspired everyone around her. Even when she needed care, she remained focused on caring for others. From her, I learned the true meaning of compassion, perseverance, and unconditional love. Her ability to find hope in the hardest of times continues to shape the way I serve others.

The Day I Received the News, and How It Changed Me

In October 2021, I received the devastating news that Rena was on a ventilator in India. I immediately began working with a team of doctors here to do whatever I could from afar. When her condition seemed to improve slightly, I decided to make a brief stop in Dubai before heading to India. But soon after, her health declined again.

While I was on my way to the hospital from the airport, just forty minutes from seeing her, I received the call. She couldn't wait for me. She was gone.

The shock of that moment is something I will never forget. The ride felt endless, as if time had stopped. Grief washed over me in waves. Her passing is etched into my heart with painful clarity—the phone call, the silence, the overwhelming weight of loss.

She was taken too soon by a disease that could have been better managed with proper access to care. That truth broke something inside me, but it also sparked a fire. I could not let this happen to someone else. I had to act.

Carrying Her Voice Forward

In the days leading up to her passing, I had a few meaningful conversations with her that brought us even closer. I still hear her voice—gentle, innocent, filled with hope and quiet courage. Despite everything she was facing, she never stopped believing in others or in better days to come.

That voice is with me still. It drives me every day in the work I do. Her strength became my strength, and her love became the foundation of a mission I could no longer ignore.

The Promise I Made to Honor Her Legacy

In the days that followed, as I grappled with my grief, I made a promise to Rena and to myself. I vowed to turn my pain into purpose—to honor her memory by dedicating my life and profession to serving those in need. This promise became the foundation of my mission and the driving force behind the creation of the Ritesh Shah Charitable Pharmacy.

There's one phone call I'll never forget — 8:14 a.m., a few days after returning from India, still reeling from losing Rena. I was sitting quietly in Freehold, unsure of what would come next, when I decided to reach out to someone who had always offered me honest guidance: Assemblyman Raj Mukherji, who today serves as a New Jersey State Senator.

What started as a check-in became a turning point. I told him about Rena's passing, about the heaviness in my chest that wouldn't lift, and about this strange stirring inside me, the feeling that I had to do something more. We talked for nearly an hour. In that call, he didn't speak like a politician or public servant. He spoke like a brother. He reminded me of what the Bhagavad Gita teaches us — about karma, about duty, and about honoring the souls who shaped us.

He told me, "If your sister inspired this feeling in you, if her memory is pulling you toward service, then that is your path. That is her blessing."

That conversation lit something in me. For the first time since her death, I felt clarity. Not ease, not peace, but purpose. And this is when the idea for Charitable Pharmacy was born.

Exactly one year later, I called him again — same time, same date — and said, "It's real now. Charitable Pharmacy exists."

He congratulated me, said he was proud, and urged me to keep pushing the vision forward.

Every prescription filled, every patient helped, is a tribute to Rena's spirit and a step toward a world where compassion and access to care are not privileges, but rights.

Rena's love continues to guide me every day. Her legacy lives on in the work I do and in the lives we touch. Through *Pills to Purpose*, I hope to share not only my journey but also the enduring power of a sister's love to inspire change and healing.

When I returned from India after losing Rena, the grief was overwhelming, but so was the clarity that followed. I knew I had to do something meaningful—not just to cope, but to make sure no one else would suffer due to lack of access to basic medication. In April 2022, we opened the Ritesh Shah Charitable Pharmacy in Red Bank, New Jersey—the first charitable pharmacy of its kind in the state. The building, painted in Rena's favorite color, green, became a symbol of healing, purpose, and service. Our mission was simple: provide free life-saving medications, immunizations, and health education to the uninsured and underinsured in our community.

The initiative quickly caught the attention of both local and national media. In an article by *Drug Store News*, the story of how Rena's passing gave rise to a movement was shared in depth. They described how the pharmacy came to life through private funding, community partnerships, and a vision rooted in love and service.

The article also highlighted our efforts in creating a comprehensive formulary, building educational programs, and reaching underserved populations, especially the working-class Latino community, many of whom suffer from diabetes but lack insurance.

Another article published by *CBS News* shed light on the broader mission of the pharmacy in the context of a broken healthcare system. The piece emphasized how our model eliminates financial barriers by removing cash registers altogether, and instead focuses on delivering compassion and medication without cost to those who would otherwise go without. I shared in that interview how the loss of my sister, a diabetic who passed away from COVID-19, shook me to the core—and how I was determined to prevent others from suffering due to a lack of access.

The impact of our work was further recognized in a feature by *Monmouth Community*, which celebrated the pharmacy surpassing $1 million in charitable donations. They documented how, with the help of dedicated volunteers and community leaders—including support from Senator Cory Booker—we've been able to distribute over $200,000 worth of insulin alone. Events like our American Pharmacist Month celebration and National Pharmacy Week breakfast have drawn support from healthcare professionals, politicians, and philanthropists, reinforcing the idea that service, when grounded in purpose, can truly move communities forward.

These articles, published in my honor, don't just tell my story—they tell Rena's. They capture the ripple effect of one promise, made in sorrow but fulfilled in hope. This journey is not about me alone; it's about every patient we've helped, every family we've supported, and every life we've touched—because of her.

Chapter 8: A Legacy of Purpose

From the very first day we opened our doors, we prioritized creating a space that felt less like a clinical setting and more like a welcoming haven. We intentionally designed the pharmacy's layout to encourage interaction. The waiting area wasn't sterile and impersonal; rather, it featured comfortable seating, soft lighting, and engaging reading materials. We fostered a relaxed atmosphere, encouraging patients to share their concerns and experiences openly, without fear of judgment. Our staff, carefully selected for their compassion and communication skills, played a pivotal role in establishing these connections. They weren't just dispensing medications; they were actively listening, offering support, and building relationships.

One story that truly shows the power of human connection is that of Mrs. Rodriguez, an elderly woman living on a fixed income who regularly struggled to afford her life-saving medications. While we were able to help with her prescriptions, it quickly became clear that her challenges went beyond just medication. She lived alone and had very little social interaction. One of our pharmacy technicians noticed how lonely she seemed and began making time to chat with her during each visit. What started as a simple conversation soon grew into a heartfelt friendship. The technician eventually began visiting Mrs. Rodriguez at home, helping with errands and offering companionship. This small act of kindness made a world of difference. Mrs. Rodriguez's emotional and mental well-being improved noticeably, and with it, so did her medication adherence. It was a powerful reminder that sometimes, healing begins with a human touch.

This experience underscored the vital role of human connection in achieving positive health outcomes. It's not merely about treating illnesses; it's about understanding the intricate web of factors affecting a person's well-being—social isolation, financial insecurity, lack of access to resources— and addressing them holistically. The human element in healthcare is not an accessory but the very cornerstone upon which our success is built.

This understanding propelled us to develop programs that explicitly focused on fostering community engagement and building relationships. We organized regular community health fairs, offering free health screenings, educational workshops, and opportunities for interaction with healthcare professionals. These events weren't just about providing services; they were about creating a sense of shared purpose, building trust, and strengthening the bonds within our community. We actively sought input from community members, incorporating their feedback into the development and implementation of our programs. This collaborative approach ensured our services were relevant and accessible, tailored to the specific needs of our diverse patient population.

The power of human connection extends beyond our direct interactions with patients. Building strong relationships with other community organizations proved invaluable. We developed partnerships with local food banks, housing assistance programs, and mental health clinics. This network of support allowed us to provide patients with comprehensive care, addressing their needs beyond the realm of medication. By working collaboratively, we were able to achieve a far greater impact than any single organization could have accomplished on its own. The referrals, the shared information, the collective understanding—all strengthened our ability to help those in need.

One striking example of this collaborative spirit involves our partnership with a local homeless shelter. We noticed a significant number of our patients were experiencing homelessness, facing immense challenges in accessing regular healthcare. Through collaboration with the shelter's staff, we established an on-site clinic, providing medication dispensing, basic health screenings, and health education programs. This initiative was transformative, not only improving the health outcomes of the shelter's residents but also strengthening our connections with this vulnerable population. We built trust, fostering a sense of community and mutual support. The stories of recovery and resilience we witnessed in this collaborative setting were profoundly moving and underscored the potential of human connection to overcome seemingly insurmountable obstacles.

The importance of human connection also extends to our staff. Creating a supportive and collaborative work environment is essential for fostering a culture of compassion and excellence. We prioritized open communication, mutual respect, and opportunities for professional development. We understood that our staff, empowered and supported, could provide the most effective and compassionate care. Team meetings weren't merely about logistical updates; they were occasions for sharing experiences, learning from each other, and reaffirming our shared commitment to serving the community. Regular training programs in empathy, communication, and cultural competency enhanced our ability to connect with patients from diverse backgrounds. By investing in our staff, we invested in the quality of our human interactions and, consequently, the effectiveness of our services.

Furthermore, we realized the importance of acknowledging and validating the emotional toll inherent in providing healthcare, particularly in a setting focused on underserved populations. We implemented stress management programs, offered access to counseling services, and fostered an environment where staff felt comfortable expressing their feelings and concerns. This commitment to our staff's well-being wasn't merely a matter of corporate responsibility; it was a recognition of the profound impact emotional exhaustion could have on the quality of care. By supporting our team, we ensured they could continue providing the compassion and understanding vital to our success.

To sum it up, the enduring power of human connection is not simply an abstract concept; it's the lifeblood of our charitable pharmacy. It's in the quiet moments of empathy, in the collaborative spirit of partnerships, in the supportive environment we foster for our staff, and in the transformative impact we have on the lives of those we serve. It is the shared humanity that transcends logistical challenges and financial constraints, driving us forward in our mission to improve the health and well-being of our community. It is this enduring power of connection that allows us to not only meet the immediate needs of our patients but also to inspire hope, build resilience, and forge a stronger, healthier community together. This unwavering commitment to fostering human connection, in all its multifaceted forms, ensures our pharmacy is not simply a place where prescriptions are dispensed but a vibrant hub where healing happens, both physically and emotionally, within the heart of our community.

This dedication translates into a multifaceted approach to mentorship and leadership development. We've established a robust mentorship program pairing experienced pharmacists and technicians with aspiring healthcare professionals from local universities and colleges. These mentorship relationships aren't confined to formal classroom settings; instead, they immerse mentees in the day-to-day realities of our pharmacy, allowing them to witness firsthand the tangible impact of compassionate care. They participate in patient interactions, observing how our team navigates complex situations, addresses patient anxieties, and provides holistic support. They learn, not just from lectures and textbooks, but from the rich tapestry of human experiences unfolding within our walls.

One of our most memorable mentorships was with Sarah, a bright and curious pharmacy student who initially felt discouraged by the gap between what she learned in the classroom and what real patients were facing. We paired her with our lead pharmacist, Dr. Anya Sharma, and that pairing changed everything. Under Dr. Sharma's guidance, Sarah quickly began to see things differently. She watched how Dr. Sharma explained complex medication routines with care and compassion—always tailoring her advice to each patient's unique situation, fears, and hopes. Sarah got involved in organizing community health fairs, spoke directly with people from all walks of life, and listened to their struggles and stories. It was eye-opening. She came to understand that pharmacy work isn't just about prescriptions—it's about people. It's about meeting them where they are, understanding their lives, and helping them navigate their health with empathy. By the time she graduated, Sarah's outlook had completely transformed. She took a job at a community clinic serving a largely underserved Latino population, where she continues to apply everything, she learned during her time with us.

Our commitment also extends to leadership development. We actively encourage our staff to participate in leadership training programs that focus on fostering ethical decision-making, conflict resolution, and collaborative team building. These aren't generic management courses; they are designed specifically to address the unique challenges of leading in a community-focused healthcare setting. We recognize that effective leadership within this context demands not just managerial competence but also the ability to inspire, motivate, and empower others to embrace a shared vision of social responsibility. We've seen our own staff flourish under this approach. Maria, a technician initially hesitant to take on additional responsibilities, has transformed into a confident leader, mentoring younger colleagues and actively participating in community outreach programs. She now spearheads our annual health fair, demonstrating exceptional organizational skills and a genuine dedication to empowering others.

Furthermore, we've partnered with several local universities to develop a specialized curriculum focused on community pharmacy and social justice. This curriculum seamlessly integrates classroom learning with hands-on experience within our pharmacy. Students participate in workshops and seminars exploring the social determinants of health, ethical dilemmas in healthcare, and effective strategies for community engagement. They also actively contribute to our pharmacy's programs, gaining invaluable experience in patient care, community outreach, and program development. This collaborative effort not only trains future healthcare professionals but also enriches our own operations, bringing fresh perspectives and innovative ideas to our team. Recent collaborations have resulted in the development of a new mobile health unit to better serve homebound patients and the creation of a culturally sensitive educational brochure series.

Beyond formal training programs, we leverage every opportunity to instill a sense of social responsibility in our workforce. We regularly share compelling stories of the patients we serve, highlighting the positive impact of compassionate care and collaborative efforts. These stories, both triumphant and challenging, underscore the importance of empathy, resilience, and unwavering commitment in facing the complexities of healthcare disparities. They inspire our staff to engage with patients deeply and humanely, shaping them into compassionate care providers. We also provide regular opportunities for staff to participate in community service initiatives outside of the pharmacy, reinforcing their commitment to civic engagement and community well-being.

Our commitment to inspiring future healthcare leaders also involves supporting research focused on addressing healthcare disparities. We actively collaborate with researchers to provide data, insights, and support for studies investigating effective strategies for improving access to care, addressing health inequities, and fostering health equity within communities. This commitment goes beyond simple data collection; we view research as a vital tool for informing policy, shaping best practices, and ultimately, driving positive change within the healthcare system.

Moreover, we understand that financial sustainability is crucial for the long-term viability of any organization, particularly one dedicated to serving vulnerable populations. Therefore, we've developed a comprehensive financial literacy program for our staff, empowering them to make informed financial decisions, manage resources effectively, and develop sustainable financial strategies for their future endeavors. This approach not only benefits our staff but also enhances our operational efficiency and financial stability, ensuring our ability to continue serving our community.

Finally, we believe that inspiring the next generation of healthcare leaders requires cultivating a mindset of continuous learning and improvement. We actively encourage our staff and mentees to engage in ongoing professional development, attend conferences, contribute to research, and pursue advanced training opportunities.

This continuous learning process ensures that we remain at the forefront of healthcare innovation, equipped with the latest knowledge and tools to address the ever-evolving needs of our community.

Our efforts to inspire future generations of healthcare leaders are intrinsically linked to the core values that define our charitable pharmacy. We are not merely dispensing medications; we are cultivating a legacy of purpose, driven by compassion, social responsibility, and a deep commitment to building a healthier and more equitable future for all. Our hope is that by nurturing a workforce steeped in these values, we can ensure that the human connection, so vital to effective healthcare, continues to thrive and serve as a guiding light for generations to come. This is the enduring legacy we aim to build – one founded on empathy, collaborative spirit, and unwavering dedication to service. It's a legacy that transcends geographical boundaries and financial limitations, empowering future generations to carry the torch of compassionate healthcare forward.

Our commitment to building a legacy of purpose extends beyond mentoring and education; it necessitates active engagement in advocacy and policy change. The systemic issues contributing to healthcare disparities—issues such as lack of insurance coverage, inadequate transportation, limited access to culturally competent care, and the pervasive influence of social determinants of health—cannot be solved by individual acts of kindness alone. These require a concerted effort at the policy level, a robust commitment to advocating for systemic change.

Our experiences at the charitable pharmacy have vividly illustrated the stark realities of healthcare inequality. We've witnessed firsthand how patients struggle to afford life-saving medications, navigate complex insurance systems, and overcome logistical barriers to accessing care. These encounters aren't just isolated incidents; they highlight a deeply ingrained systemic problem demanding immediate attention and transformative solutions. We've seen patients making impossible choices – skipping meals to afford their insulin, foregoing essential medical appointments due to transportation limitations, or delaying treatment because of the prohibitive cost of prescription drugs.

This understanding has fueled our deep involvement in policy advocacy. We recognize that true and lasting change necessitates influencing the very structures that perpetuate healthcare disparities. This involves more than just expressing our concerns; it demands active participation in the policy-making process.

Our advocacy efforts have taken various forms. We've actively participated in legislative initiatives aimed at expanding healthcare access, particularly focusing on programs that directly address the needs of the underserved. For example, we supported the passage of a state bill that increased funding for community health clinics, recognizing that these clinics often serve as the primary point of care for vulnerable populations. We testified before legislative committees, sharing our firsthand accounts of the challenges faced by our patients and advocating for policies that would alleviate their burdens. Our testimony wasn't simply a recitation of statistics; it was a heartfelt narrative filled with compelling stories that humanized the data, making the impact of policy decisions tangible for lawmakers. We've shared stories like that of Mrs. Rodriguez, a diabetic patient who, despite her meticulous adherence to her treatment plan, faced constant anxieties about affording her insulin. Her story, and others like it, resonated deeply with policymakers, motivating them to support measures that improve medication affordability.

Beyond legislative advocacy, we've been deeply involved in grassroots efforts to spark real change. We've hosted community forums that not only raise awareness about healthcare disparities but also give people the tools and confidence to speak up and advocate for themselves and others. These gatherings have become spaces where stories are shared, connections are made, and a sense of shared responsibility is built. By teaming up with local organizations that champion social justice and health equity, we've formed a strong and united front. These partnerships have helped us reach more people and make a bigger impact. Together, we've been able to rally community support around the policies that truly matter, bringing more voices to the table and pushing for changes that reflect the needs of those most affected.

We also recognize the crucial role of public awareness. We've utilized various channels to raise public awareness about healthcare disparities and the urgent need for reform. This includes publishing articles in local newspapers and health journals, sharing our experiences on social media, and presenting at conferences and workshops. The goal is to foster a broader societal understanding of the challenges faced by underserved populations, inspiring wider support for policy solutions. We've made it a point to emphasize the human cost of inaction, sharing stories of patients whose lives have been irrevocably altered by lack of access to adequate healthcare. This approach aims to evoke empathy and motivate individuals to demand systemic change.

Another key aspect of our advocacy strategy involves actively engaging with policymakers. We've built relationships with legislators, providing them with valuable insights into the lived experiences of our patients. This isn't about lobbying for special interests; it's about providing policymakers with accurate, on-the-ground information to inform better policy decisions. This involves regularly meeting with representatives, participating in town halls, and offering our expertise in the development of healthcare-related legislation. We've found that by building trust and fostering collaborative relationships, we can more effectively influence policy decisions.

Furthermore, we believe that data is crucial for effective advocacy. We have meticulously documented the experiences of our patients, analyzing the trends and patterns that reveal the systemic nature of healthcare disparities. This data informs our advocacy efforts, providing concrete evidence to support our claims and reinforce our arguments for policy change. We've shared this data with policymakers, researchers, and community organizations, contributing to a broader body of knowledge that can inform effective strategies for addressing healthcare disparities. This commitment to data-driven advocacy strengthens our credibility and empowers us to make evidence-based recommendations for policy reform.

Our advocacy extends beyond immediate legislative concerns; it also involves advocating for long-term systemic changes. We understand that simply addressing symptoms isn't enough. We must address the root causes of health inequities. This means advocating for policies that promote social justice, address poverty and housing insecurity, improve access to education and job training, and enhance community infrastructure. We recognize that health is not merely the absence of disease but is interwoven with broader societal factors. We've actively supported initiatives aimed at improving transportation access, expanding affordable housing options, and fostering economic development in underserved neighborhoods.

We also actively participate in the development and implementation of health equity initiatives. This includes collaborating with local health departments and community organizations to create innovative programs aimed at improving health outcomes for underserved populations. For example, we partnered with a local non-profit to develop a mobile health clinic that provides essential healthcare services to individuals in remote and underserved areas. This collaborative approach not only delivers immediate care but also creates a model for replicating successful interventions elsewhere. We've also worked with community organizations to develop culturally sensitive health education programs, tailored to the specific needs and preferences of diverse populations.

Our commitment to advocacy and policy change is an ongoing journey. It requires consistent effort, resilience, and a deep belief in the transformative power of collective action.

We recognize that lasting change doesn't happen overnight, but we remain firmly committed to working towards a healthcare system that is just, equitable, and accessible to all. Our legacy will not be defined solely by the number of patients we serve within the four walls of our charitable pharmacy, but also by the systemic changes we help create to ensure that future generations have access to the healthcare they deserve. This commitment to advocacy is not merely a secondary endeavor; it is the essential complement to our direct patient care, an indispensable component of our legacy of purpose. It is through this sustained commitment to advocacy and policy change that we hope to build a healthier, more equitable future for all. This is the legacy we aim to leave behind – a world where compassionate care is not merely an ideal, but a universally accessible reality.

The closure of the charitable pharmacy, though bittersweet, marks not an end but a potential beginning. The seeds of hope we planted, the relationships we fostered, and the systems we helped strengthen are far from wilting. In fact, the legacy we aim to leave behind extends far beyond the walls of that small space. Our hope is that the model we established – a blend of compassionate care, accessible services, and community engagement – will inspire similar initiatives in other underserved areas.

One patient, a single mother of three struggling with a chronic illness, embodies this indomitable spirit. Diagnosed with type 2 diabetes at a young age, she faced numerous financial and logistical challenges in managing her condition. The cost of medication was a significant burden, and accessing specialized care proved difficult. Through our program, she not only received affordable medication but also gained access to nutritional counseling, diabetes education, and a supportive network of other patients facing similar challenges. Her journey exemplifies the transformative power of integrated care and the importance of addressing the multifaceted needs of vulnerable populations. Over time, she became a vocal advocate for our services, sharing her story and helping us connect with other individuals in need. Her resilience and unwavering determination to improve her health and the lives of her children were nothing short of inspiring.

This story, therefore, is not merely an account of a charitable pharmacy; it is a narrative of hope, demonstrating the potential for transformative change when compassion, purpose, and community coalesce. It's a story that hopefully inspires readers to consider their own potential to contribute to the well-being of others and to seek out their unique purpose in making a positive impact on the world. The human spirit, as demonstrated throughout this journey, possesses an almost limitless capacity for resilience, compassion, and positive change. Let this be a testament to that enduring truth. The world needs more individuals and organizations committed to addressing social inequities, and this journey serves as a testament to the tangible and meaningful impact that can be achieved through collaborative effort and a commitment to serving others. The journey of the charitable pharmacy is, in essence, a journey of hope, a testament to the power of the human spirit, and a blueprint for creating a more just and equitable world. It's a reminder that even small acts of compassion can create ripples of positive change, impacting not only individual lives but the entire community. The lasting legacy of the charitable pharmacy, therefore, is not just the services provided but the inspiration it offers to others to embark on similar journeys of purpose and compassion.

The strength of the community spirit also manifested in the

remarkable generosity and dedication of our volunteers.

From medical professionals donating their expertise to university students contributing their time and energy, every individual played a critical role in our success. Their commitment to our mission underscored the power of shared purpose and the capacity of individuals to come together to solve complex problems. Their willingness to go above and beyond, often sacrificing their personal time and resources, highlighted the deeply ingrained compassion within our community. Many of our volunteers developed lasting relationships with patients, forging bonds based on mutual respect and understanding that extend well beyond the confines of our service.

Moreover, the collaborative relationships we built with other community organizations proved crucial. By working alongside food banks, housing agencies, and job training programs, we created a holistic approach to healthcare that addressed the complex interplay of social and medical factors. This inter-agency collaboration proved far more effective than a piecemeal approach, demonstrating the value of integrated care and the power of synergy when diverse organizations work together with a shared vision. The collaborative nature of our efforts extended not only to other organizations but also to our relationships with patients, empowering them to become active participants in their own healthcare journey. We encouraged patient feedback and incorporated it into our service delivery model, creating a cycle of continuous improvement and mutual learning.

The data we gathered over the course of our work gave us more than just numbers. It offered a real window into the struggles many underserved communities face when it comes to healthcare. Each data point reflected someone's story, their challenges, and their hopes. These insights became the foundation of our advocacy, helping us back up our funding requests and push for policy changes with solid, real-world evidence. More importantly, the data showed how effective our integrated care model could be. By grounding our efforts in the lived experiences of the people we serve, we made sure our voice was not just heard, but taken seriously in the fight for better healthcare access for everyone.

The sustainable model we established—one based on diverse funding streams, strong partnerships, and community engagement—offers a replicable framework for other communities seeking to address healthcare disparities. The meticulous documentation of our experiences, including our operational procedures, funding strategies, partnership models, and community engagement initiatives, serves as a valuable resource for those seeking to create similar programs. Our aim was not to create a singular success story, but rather a blueprint that can be adapted and adopted by others striving to address the urgent need for accessible and compassionate healthcare in underserved communities. We believe that our approach can serve as a model for positive and sustainable change.

Reflecting on the journey of the charitable pharmacy, the most enduring legacy is the profound impact on the human spirit. It's a testament to the transformative power of purpose, resilience, and community. It's a story of hope, demonstrating that even in the face of overwhelming challenges, meaningful and sustainable change is possible. The unwavering commitment of our team, volunteers, partners, and patients showcases the incredible potential for collaboration and the extraordinary power of human compassion. The success of this endeavor wasn't simply a matter of providing medication; it was about fostering connections, building community, and empowering individuals to take control of their health and their future.

The lessons learned throughout this endeavor are not only relevant to the field of healthcare but extend far beyond it.

Chapter 9: Charitable Pharmacy and Becoming America's Pharmacist

It was a cold evening in December 2007 when I locked the doors of Bayshore Homecare Pharmacy—my very first drugstore, which Asha and I had just opened. It had been another long day. I was exhausted and ready to head home. As I turned off the lights and punched in the code to set the alarm, the phone rang.

I hesitated for a moment, debating whether to answer—but something told me I should.

On the other end was a frail, trembling voice—an elderly woman named Margaret, who had been battling cancer. She apologized for calling so late and explained that she had run out of her pain medication. She didn't have the money to pay for it.

She was waiting for a government check that hadn't arrived yet. Tears filled her voice as she described how unbearable the pain had become.

I closed my eyes and gripped the phone, feeling the weight of her desperation sink into my chest. I could hear the hopelessness in her words—the way she spoke as if she didn't expect anyone to care.

A lump formed in my throat. I knew exactly what I had to do.

Without hesitation, I told her, "Don't worry, Margaret, I'll bring the medication to you."

She gasped, as if kindness was something she hadn't felt in a long time.

"You will?" she whispered, barely believing it.

"Yes," I said firmly. "Just hang in there. I'll be there soon." She started to cry, thanking me between sobs, and I had to swallow my own emotions just to keep my voice steady.

I unlocked the pharmacy door and turned the lights back on. The cash register was closed, and the register wouldn't match the next day if I gave away medicine for free.

But none of that mattered—Margaret mattered.

I quickly filled her prescription, grabbed my coat, and stepped into the freezing night air.

The roads were quiet on Beer's Street once you passed the bayshore hospital, and the cold seeped through my jacket, but all I could think about was getting to her as fast as I could.

When I arrived at her small apartment, I knocked lightly. Her grandson, Gene, who is also not 100% well, opens the door.

The door opened slowly, revealing a fragile woman wrapped in a thin blanket, side by her grandson, and her eyes sunken but filled with gratitude.

She looked at me like I was some kind of angel, but I was just a pharmacist doing what I knew was right.

"You didn't have to do this," she said, with lots of emotion, love, and gratitude.

"Yes, I did," I told her, placing the bag of medication in her trembling hands.

She clutched it like it was the most precious gift she had ever received.

Then, to my surprise, she reached out and gently held my hand.

"No one... no one has ever done something like this for me before," she whispered.

Tears welled up in my eyes, but I fought them back.

"Everyone deserves to be cared for," I said softly.

She nodded, pressing the bag to her chest as if it held hope itself.

"I don't know how to repay you," she said, looking ashamed. "There's nothing to repay," I assured her. "Just take your medicine and rest."

She smiled—a weak, tired smile—but it was the most genuine smile I had seen in a long time.

As I turned to leave, she called out, "You have no idea what this means to me."

I paused at the door, taking a deep breath.

"I think I do," I said before stepping back into the cold night. The drive home felt different—as if the world was a little warmer, a little kinder.

I didn't care about the money, the loss, or the late hour.

All I cared about was that somewhere, in a small apartment, Margaret was resting, her pain eased, her heart a little lighter.

That night, I lay in bed, staring at the ceiling, thinking about purpose.

Pharmacy was never just about prescriptions to me—it was about people. Each bottle, each pill, represented a chance to touch a life, to be a part of someone's narrative.

It was about compassion, humanity, and doing the right thing when no one was watching.

Margaret's voice stayed with me, and her gratitude remained in my mind. I knew I would never forget that moment.

I remember explaining to my kids why Dad was late for dinner that night. Sar was about 10, and Krina was 6. It had become part of our bedtime routine. As I tucked them in, I often shared stories from the life of a pharmacist—stories about their parents and the privilege we have of working with patients every day.

They loved those bedtime stories. They were always eager to hear about helping people and making a difference, even in small and simple ways.

Years later, when I opened Ritesh Shah Charitable Pharmacy, I thought of Margaret.

She was one of the many reasons I vowed to serve those who had nowhere else to turn.

It wasn't just about medicine—it was about giving people dignity, hope, and kindness.

And as long as I could, I would continue doing exactly that. Because that night in 2007 wasn't just about helping a patient—it was about discovering the true meaning of service.

March 2017 – Katrina Thompson

A Life Saved, A Purpose Found

Life was busy at the time, and everything seemed to be moving in fast forward.

It was a quiet morning at the pharmacy when Katrina walked in, pale and struggling to breathe. Her hands trembled as she gripped the counter, her voice barely audible.

"Something's wrong," she whispered.

I looked into her eyes just as she started to collapse toward me.

I had seen countless patients before, but something about her urgency made me stop in my tracks. I quickly assessed her symptoms: labored breathing, dizziness, and confusion. Years of experience took over. I checked her blood pressure, and it was dangerously low.

I asked Leo, my clerk, to run next door to Gem's Bagels and grab some salt. As I asked her a few quick questions, I had a gut feeling. I opened the refrigerator and took out a Sprite, thinking it might be her blood sugar or maybe her blood pressure. Whatever it was, I knew we had to act fast.

Without hesitation, I acted. Calling 911 while offering immediate assistance, I tried to stabilize her as best as I could until paramedics arrived. The minutes stretched into eternity, but by the time she was wheeled out. I don't know what happened after that, but a few days later, when I was opening up my drugstore, I saw a few reporters and news channel reporters saying, *Who is Ritesh Shah? Why are they calling him a hero?* Confused and curious, when I replied, "Ritesh," the reporter asked me, "Did you know you saved a patient's life?" I was taken aback. Saved her life? Immediately, I realized what had happened two days ago. I also got a call from Bayshore Hospital explaining what happened with her.

She was suffering from a sudden episode of severe pulmonary embolism, and my quick thinking to offer an immediate sugar & salt boost had stabilized her until further medical help.

Days later, she walked back in—not as a patient, but as a friend, gratitude shining in her eyes. "You saved my life," she said.

For me, that moment wasn't just about saving a life. It was about purpose—about why I had become a pharmacist in the first place. That purpose…

Because sometimes, a single moment can change everything. It can be unexpectedly profound; it bridges the distance between mere routine and a genuine calling.

Understanding the patient's situation has always been eye-opening for me. Another incident at the pharmacy helped to stress that sometimes falling a few dollars short for a co-pay can be life-threatening, especially for diabetes or blood clot prevention meds.

The Price of Life

It was just another routine evening at the pharmacy—until she walked in. An elderly woman, frail yet determined, slid a prescription across the counter. I glanced at it: Lovenox. A life-saving blood thinner. Essential. Non-negotiable.

I processed her insurance, and then the total appeared on the screen. When I told her the copay, her face fell. She reached into her worn-out purse, counting crumpled bills and loose change. She was a few dollars short.

"I'll come back tomorrow," she murmured, turning away. But I knew the truth—there might not be a tomorrow if she missed this dose. A clot could form. A stroke. A heart attack. All for the sake of a few dollars.

At that moment, something shifted inside me. This wasn't just about medicine. This was about humanity. Without a second thought, I handed her the medication and simply said, "Take it. Your health comes first." Her eyes welled up with tears as she whispered, "God bless you."

That day, I realized that access to medication shouldn't be a privilege—it should be a right. That moment stayed with me, fueling a mission that would one day lead to the creation of a charitable pharmacy. Because no one should ever have to choose between their life and their wallet.

Keansburg - Feb 8, 2018 - true and live patient testimonial -

what a pharmacist does every day to serve patients. It's a story about a patient who came to the pharmacy to inform me about our staff pharmacist, Nirav Patel, who did something extraordinary, which is way beyond the normal courtesy of a pharmacist.

Nirav delivered a medication to the patient during heavy rain and snow in the blizzard in the worst conditions, and not only that, he sat down with the patient and explained to her what was going on with her nebulizer medication and how to use it. If the patient had not gotten this medication, she would have been back in the hospital. For her husband to come and express his gratitude towards the profession, as well as what it meant for him. Seeing not only what I do every day, but seeing other fellow pharmacists doing and going way beyond was very inspiring and special. It reinforced my belief that the heart of healthcare lies in genuine compassion and selflessness.

Planting Seeds of Purpose: A Day at Bayshore Senior Center

April 14th, 2016, was more than just another day at the pharmacy — it was a reflection of a promise I had made years ago, born from a place of deep personal pain.

It was a quiet morning in April 2016 at the Bayshore Senior Center in Keansburg. One of my students, Matthew Cheung—a PharmD candidate from Rutgers University—stood before a room of seniors in his white coat, speaking with confidence and care. His topic was diabetes, but his message carried something deeper: compassion, understanding, and hope.

I had the privilege of being Matthew's preceptor during his clinical rotation at Drugsmart Pharmacy. But mentoring students was never just about pharmacology or fulfilling academic requirements. It was about passing on the deeper "why" of our profession—why we show up, why we serve, why we care.

For me, diabetes has always been personal. It wasn't just a condition I studied; it was the disease that consumed my father's health. I grew up watching him struggle with daily finger pricks, low blood sugar crashes, and a quiet, dignified suffering that marked much of his later life. I can still remember the fear in my mother's eyes as she rushed to get him juice during a sudden episode, and the helplessness I felt as a son who couldn't fix it.

That helplessness planted a seed, a promise that one day, I'd find a way to help others avoid the pain my father endured.

So as Matthew spoke, explaining blood sugar control, medications, nutrition, and habits, I stood off to the side, watching our seniors listen with wide, curious eyes. Some asked questions; others just nodded slowly, taking it all in. I could tell these weren't just new facts to them—they were lifelines. And when I added in real stories about my father and the consequences of unmanaged diabetes, I saw the fear in their eyes too, but also the motivation. Sometimes, fear can be the catalyst for change.

That day wasn't just about health education. It was about restoring dignity. It was about honoring a promise I made long ago. It was about legacy—not just mine, but my father's. His story now lives on through my students, through every patient we touched, and through every moment where compassion turned into action.

We don't get to choose the pain life gives us, but we do get to choose what we do with it.

That day at Bayshore, I chose to turn pain into purpose. And I watched that purpose take root, one heartfelt conversation at a time.

A Personal Message to You — and to Myself

If you're reading this and you have a loved one living with diabetes—or you're living with it yourself—I want you to know something very important:

You are not alone.

I've lived the fear, and I am living with diabetes. I do get frustrated. But now that has been prevented? I've lived the frustration. I've lived the helplessness of watching someone you love battle a disease without the tools or support to fight back. It is a pain that leaves a mark—but it's also a pain that has shaped my purpose.

But here's what I've learned:

Knowledge is power.

As a pharmacist, I've been blessed with the knowledge to understand my condition, and as a father to a caring son who's now a doctor, I'm reminded that our legacy can be one of healing. Education doesn't just help manage diabetes—it helps us rise above the fear and gives us the strength to empower others.

Education is freedom.

It may not cure diabetes, but it gives us the tools to live better, to suffer less, and to share what we know. When we choose to lean into understanding, we transform the burden into something meaningful—something we can pass on with love.

Support is everything.

I want to pause here because this part is everything to me. My purpose, my strength, my ability to keep going… none of it would exist without my family.

Asha, my wife, is my anchor. Her gentle reassurances, her unwavering love, her quiet strength, she is the reason I'm still standing.

Krina, my daughter, is the light in my day. Her optimism lifts me in moments when I feel low. Her joyful spirit reminds me that life is still beautiful, even when it's hard.

Sarthak, my son, is my steady compass. His wisdom, calm presence, and quiet willingness to step up without being asked ground me, especially on days when I feel overwhelmed.

They are not just part of my life. They are the reason I'm living it with purpose.

So, to you, whether you're managing diabetes, supporting someone who is, or simply trying to make sense of it all, know this:

There is strength in knowledge.
There is hope in support.
And there is healing in love.

You are not alone.
Neither am I.

We cannot change the past, but we can shape the future — one conversation, one choice, one act of care at a time.

Please, never underestimate the power you hold to make a difference.

Sometimes, the smallest moments can spark the greatest healing. Whether it's asking a thoughtful question, offering a kind word, or helping someone understand their medications, it matters.

My father's story became my purpose.

Inspired by his struggles, I made it my mission to reach seniors in our community. It started with a simple, heartfelt presentation at the Bayshore Senior Center.

Maybe, by reading this, a part of your story is also beginning to find its purpose.

Keep going. Keep giving. Keep planting seeds of hope.

A Moment of Connection: Betty James and the Gift of Care

April 26th, 2018 — another day where purpose met practice.

At a Bingo community event that afternoon, I had the honor of connecting with Betty James, a sweet and spirited senior who reminded me so much of the patients I promised to serve when I first put on my pharmacist coat with Nelly, my pharmacist from Bayshore, who was helping me.

We weren't just playing Bingo that day.

We were hosting a diabetes education class woven into the event, finding creative ways to reach seniors where they were, on their terms, in their community.

As I handed Betty a small prize, I realized it wasn't about what was inside the box. It was about the message behind it: "We see you. We care about you. We are here to help you live a healthier life."

Seniors like Betty deserve more than lectures and pamphlets. They deserve conversations. They deserve patience. They deserve trust.

Many of them have been quietly managing diabetes for years,

often feeling forgotten, overwhelmed, or alone.

I knew, from watching my own father's struggles, that a few simple tools — education, encouragement, and consistency— could change not only numbers on a chart, but years on a life.

Moments like this are the heart of my mission:

To empower seniors to live healthier, fuller lives despite diabetes.

To meet them where they are — in community rooms, at Bingo tables, during moments of laughter and connection. To make health education feel human, not clinical.

Moments like Bayshore were just the beginning. Two years later, I found myself at a community Bingo event, continuing to sow the seeds of education and hope, one senior at a time.

Looking at Betty's smile that day, I knew:

The seeds we plant with love and service always find a way to grow. And we didn't stop there.

Every small act had a purpose.

Mixing children's liquid medications and adding flavors they loved wasn't just about making it easier for them to take their medicine — it was about easing their struggles, bringing them comfort, and helping them heal without fear.

Measuring patients and fitting them for compression stockings, whether it was for varicose veins or swelling from heart conditions, wasn't just another task — it was a chance to improve their quality of life, to give them hope in their everyday steps. Visits to local community centers were not merely social calls but rich experiences where lives were altered.

Delivering medications at no cost to seniors and handicapped patients, especially through brutally cold winters, wasn't just a service — it was Seva, the purest form of giving without expecting anything in return.

For over twenty years, moments like these — small in the eyes of the world, but monumental in the hearts of those we served — slowly shaped the foundation of my purpose.

They taught me that true pharmacy was never just about filling prescriptions. It was about touching lives. Each interaction was an opportunity to connect, to uplift, to make a difference beyond the confines of medicine.

It was about filling lives with dignity, kindness, and care.

It was these very seeds of service that eventually led me to a greater mission — the creation of a charitable pharmacy, where compassion could finally be prescribed without barriers. We started this endeavor in an old, modest building, where hope and healing flowed more abundantly than funds.

There are moments in a pharmacist's life that go far beyond counting pills or counseling patients.

One of those moments came during a delivery to Dr. Gopal's office. Dr Krish Gopal, whom I have known for 20 years now, taught me so much about love, compassion, and kindness. He is one of the most humble people I have ever met in my life. As an oncologist, he greeted every patient with warmth, always taking the time to truly listen to their stories. He never rushed, never dismissed — he cared with his whole heart, both as a physician and as a human being.

That day, one of his cancer patients was undergoing chemotherapy. She was frail, fighting, and quietly courageous. She was waiting for her Neulasta injection, along with pain patches to ease the harsh side effects of her treatment.

I arrived with the medications, but something unexpected happened.

The pain patches, which were supposed to bring her some comfort, wouldn't stick properly to her skin.

Her body, weakened and sensitive from the treatments, simply couldn't hold them. And in that moment, it wasn't enough to just hand over the medications and walk away.

I rushed back to the pharmacy, searching for nonstick medical tape — anything that could help secure the patches to her body, so she wouldn't have to suffer another unnecessary layer of pain.

Returning to her, I gently showed her and the nurse how to use the tape to place the patches securely on her arm and upper chest, making sure they would stay in place and do their job.

For over twenty years, moments like these — small in the eyes of the world, but monumental in the hearts of those we served — slowly shaped the foundation of my purpose.

They taught me that true pharmacy was never just about filling prescriptions.

It was about filling lives with dignity, compassion, and care.

It was these very seeds of service that eventually led me to a greater mission — the creation of a charitable pharmacy, where compassion could finally be prescribed without barriers.

Medicine Man

October 2024 - Monmouth Magazine

The day the Monmouth Magazine article titled "Medicine Man" was published, I found myself reflecting on the journey that brought me to that moment—a journey shaped by loss, resilience, and an unwavering commitment to service. Being recognized in Monmouth Magazine was more than a personal honor; it was a testament to the collective spirit of everyone who believed in the mission of the Ritesh Shah Charitable Pharmacy. The article captured the heart of our work: fighting healthcare inequities, one life-saving prescription at a time.

The story began with my family's own struggles and sacrifices. My wife, Asha, and I were both trained as pharmacists, and together we navigated the challenges of building a life in a new country. The turning point came in October 2021, when I traveled to India to see my sister, Rena, only to lose her to COVID-19 complications before I could say goodbye. Her passing shook me to my core. I returned to New Jersey with a sense of purpose I had never known. I told Asha, "We need to do more." That conviction became the foundation for the first charitable pharmacy in New Jersey—a place where no one would be denied medication because of their circumstances.

The article described how our pharmacy operates without a cash register—every life-saving medication is free of charge. We built a formulary of over 180 essential medications, focusing on diabetes, heart disease, mental health, and nutrition. We partnered with local clinics like Parker Family Health Center, faith-based organizations, and community groups to ensure that patients who needed help the most could find us. Our approach was simple: treat every patient with dignity, educate before we medicate, and build a healthier community by addressing the root causes of health disparities.

Recognition from the magazine—and from the broader community—was humbling. It wasn't just about me; it was about the movement we started together. The article highlighted stories of patients who no longer had to choose between food and medicine, of volunteers who found new purpose in service, and of my wife, Asha, who joined me as our pharmacy's trustee and pharmacist-in-charge, serving without compensation. It also acknowledged the support of friends, partners, and organizations who believed in our vision and helped make it a reality.

Being called a "Medicine Man" was a reminder that this work is sacred. Every prescription filled, every patient counseled, every life touched is a tribute to my sister's memory and a promise to my community. The magazine feature wasn't just a milestone in my career—it was a celebration of hope, compassion, and the belief that one person's purpose can ignite change for hundreds.

It reaffirmed my commitment to keep going, to keep serving, and to keep shining Rena's light in every corner of Monmouth County and beyond.

I often thought—Medicine Man sounds like Spider-Man.

What did I do to deserve this? How did life become this way?

Chapter 10:
See in Mom's Eyes – Peace and a
Stronger Purpose

When I think about where my discipline and drive came from, it started much earlier than pharmacy school; it started with my mother.

Back when I was in my 10th to 12th grade and first year of college, trying to figure out how I would survive the pressures of this new world, my mom would quietly wake up with me in the early morning hours. While I buried myself in textbooks, she would sit nearby with her *prarthana* book in hand, reading her daily prayers softly so as not to disturb me. She never said much, but her presence was steady like a quiet anchor during the storm.

I didn't understand it then the way I do now. I thought I was the only one sacrificing sleep, pushing myself, doing what had to be done. But she was there too, every morning, eyes tired, back aching, but refusing to let me study alone. She would make tea, light the incense, and sometimes glance over just to make sure I hadn't fallen asleep over my notes. That routine became our rhythm.

Her faith gave me strength before I had any of my own. Her belief that I could become something, that I could rise up and serve others, became the foundation I stood on when I struggled the most.

There was a moment of quiet peace that I will never forget. When my mother traveled all the way from India to visit the Ritesh Shah Charitable Pharmacy, she watched as patients received the care and medications they so desperately needed. I could see the emotion in her eyes as she took in the scene—the shelves stocked with hope, the smiles of relief on patients' faces, and the gentle hum of service in action.

After a while, she turned to me, her voice soft but full of conviction, and said, "Only this brother could do this." In her words, I heard not just pride, but a deep sense of understanding and peace. In that moment, it felt as though she truly saw the purpose behind my journey—the healing, the giving, and the honoring of family.

That simple sentence from my mother was a quiet blessing. It reminded me that Pills to Purpose was never just about medicine or charity. It was about bringing peace to my own heart and to those I serve. It was about turning pain into purpose and fulfilling a promise that began with love and loss.

My mother's presence at the pharmacy made my purpose even stronger. Seeing the impact firsthand, she knows that no one—whether one person or thousands—should lose a loved one simply because they couldn't access the medications they needed. For her, this is the most meaningful way her son could honor his baby sister's memory.

I carry this moment with me every day, and I think about it with every prescription I dispense. It is a constant reminder that this mission is bigger than me. It is a legacy of love, hope, and healing. Every pill and every interaction is a step toward ensuring that compassion continues to win.

The Ripple Effect: How Medication Access Transforms Families

Jose Sanchez, a 47-year-old landscaper from Long Branch, depends on seasonal work and lives with diabetes and high blood pressure. For him, the Ritesh Shah Charitable Pharmacy is nothing short of a godsend. By receiving his medications through our pharmacy, he now saves $740 a month—enough to help cover rent and buy groceries for his family.

Access to medication is more than just a healthcare issue; it is a lifeline that touches every corner of a family's world. When a loved one can get the medicine they need, it brings a sense of relief that's hard to put into words. It means fewer sleepless nights spent worrying, fewer emergency room visits, and more moments of peace and normalcy.

For many families, medications are the bridge between illness and health, between fear and hope. When that bridge is missing or broken, families face impossible choices—deciding whether to pay for life-saving medicine or put food on the table, choosing between their own well-being and that of their loved ones. These are not just financial decisions; they are heart-wrenching dilemmas that weigh heavily on parents, spouses, and children alike.

Medication access empowers families to become active partners in healing. It allows them to care for their loved ones with confidence, manage chronic conditions without constant crisis, and envision a future where illness does not define their lives. It strengthens the bonds of family by reducing stress and restoring hope.

When a pharmacy like ours provides medications free of charge, it sends a powerful message: you are not alone. Your health matters. Your family matters. This simple act of access transforms despair into dignity, fear into faith, and isolation into community.

Every prescription we dispense carries with it the promise of a better tomorrow—not just for one patient, but for the entire family whose lives are connected to theirs. This is why our mission is about far more than pills; it is about healing families, restoring hope, and building a legacy of compassion.

Jose's wife, who often comes by the pharmacy to pick up his medications, works part-time as a kitchen helper in a Mexican restaurant to make ends meet. She once told me, "These medicines keep him healthy—and not just that—they keep our family together. The stress of paying for medication is gone." Her words and blessings mean the world to me, and I am sure they would make my sister proud.

We've witnessed incredible transformations when these medicines reach the hands of those in need. And each time, we are reminded that healing begins not just in the body, but in the hearts of families who can now live with one less burden.

When the Ritesh Shah Charitable Pharmacy opened its doors in Red Bank on Good Friday in April 2022, the timing held a profound symbolism. As Rev. Terrence Porter of Pilgrim Baptist Church observed, "A Hindu by religion couple opens up a door of a charitable pharmacy in a highly dense Christian faith community on the eve of Passover observed by Jewish on Good Friday in the holy month of Ramadan." His words captured the spirit of unity and service that defined that moment.

This convergence of faiths and traditions was more than a coincidence; it was a powerful reminder that compassion knows no boundaries. The pharmacy, founded and self-funded by my wife and me, was created to serve all patients, regardless of background or belief. Our mission has always been to increase access to medications and care for the uninsured and underserved, helping reduce health inequities in our community.

Opening the pharmacy during such a meaningful intersection of religious observances sent a clear message: every person, from every walk of life, is welcome and valued here. In that moment, faiths and cultures came together for a single purpose—to heal, to serve, and to uplift those in need. That is the true heart of our work, and it continues to guide us with every prescription we fill.

All these blessings and meaningful messages only strengthened my determination. It felt as though each endorsement and each symbol of faith added to our resolve and deepened our commitment to this mission.

By June 2022—just three months after we opened—we had already started making an impact. And that's the purpose.

Every day at the pharmacy, I'm reminded that our work is about far more than dispensing medication. It's about restoring hope, dignity, and life itself. These moments unfold in real time, right in front of us, and they shape not only the futures of our patients but also our own sense of purpose as pharmacists.

Take April Santiago, for example. She came to us facing an impossible decision: buy her eight essential medications or put food on the table for her family. When she told us, "If you were not here, I would have been dead. Between you and Parker Clinic, now I have hope that I will be able to survive and live," it stopped me in my tracks.

Hope—isn't that a wonderful word? Now, when April walks into our pharmacy, she does so with a peaceful heart and a smile that reminds us why we do what we do.

Then there's Jose Luna, a diabetic patient who was forced to ration his insulin because he simply couldn't afford the $300 monthly cost. Insulin is not a luxury—it's a necessity, a lifeline. Watching Jose's relief when he learned he could receive his insulin free of charge at our pharmacy was a powerful reminder of the impact we can have. No one should have to risk their life or health because they can't afford their medication.

These stories play out daily at our pharmacy counter, turning each day into a testament of resilience and compassion. They create hope not only in the lives of our patients, but in ours as well. Every story renews my commitment to the oath I took as a pharmacist and affirms that our mission—turning pills into purpose—is real, and it's working, one patient at a time.

And these are just two stories. I know there will be many more in the months and years ahead, each one a new chapter in our ongoing journey of service and hope, with purpose at its core.

April Santiago's presence had a deeply uplifting effect on the morale of our pharmacy staff. Her transformation—from someone forced to choose between food and medicine to a patient who now walks in singing and offering heartfelt blessings—became a daily source of inspiration.

Encounters like April's serve as powerful reminders of the real-life impact of our work. They highlight the deeper meaning behind what we do and help foster empathy, pride, and a renewed sense of commitment to patient care. Her hope and joy were contagious, uplifting the entire team and reinforcing the sense of purpose that makes every day at the pharmacy more meaningful.

Chapter 11: Building a Sustainable Organization

The transformation of our pharmacy wasn't solely about internal changes; it also required a fundamental shift in our approach to resource management and fundraising.

Providing free or heavily subsidized healthcare services to a vulnerable population requires a robust and sustainable financial model. This wasn't simply about balancing the books; it was about ensuring the long-term viability of our mission to serve the community. At first, the challenges felt overwhelming. Our existing resources were insufficient to cover the expanding scope of our services, particularly the increased demand for medication assistance and the implementation of our new patient support programs.

Our fundraising strategy was multifaceted, embracing a blend of sponsorships and community-based initiatives. Securing grants proved to be a complex undertaking, requiring meticulous proposal writing, strong storytelling that captured the impact of our work, and a demonstrable track record of success. We invested considerable time and effort in developing compelling grant applications, clearly articulating our mission, the needs of our community, our impact metrics, and our long-term goals. We focused on foundations and organizations aligned with our mission, seeking grants specifically designated for community health initiatives, medication assistance programs, and patient support services. The process involved multiple revisions, detailed budget justifications, and persistent follow-up. The rejection letters were frequent and, at times, disheartening, but each one pushed us to sharpen our focus and improve our applications.

Beyond grant applications, we actively cultivated individual donations. We launched a website with a dedicated donation page, making it easy for individuals to contribute securely online. We also utilized traditional methods such as direct mail campaigns and flyers distributed in the community, sharing real patient stories to create an emotional connection with donors.

We organized a series of fundraising events throughout the year, from small-scale coffee mornings to larger galas, fostering a sense of community engagement and providing opportunities for donors to interact with our staff and patients. Transparency was crucial; we meticulously documented how donations were used, ensuring donors felt confident that their contributions were directly impacting the lives of those we served. We also instituted a regular newsletter that detailed the positive impact of their support and showcased how their generosity made a difference. Stories of patients who had received life-saving medications or benefitted from our services offered living proof of the effectiveness of our mission.

Our efforts extended to cultivating corporate sponsorships. We approached local businesses, explaining how a partnership with us would not only enhance their corporate social responsibility profile but also provide a valuable return on investment. We proposed a variety of sponsorship options, tailored to different budget levels and offering varying degrees of visibility and engagement. Some sponsorships involved providing financial contributions, while others involved in-kind donations such as office supplies, printing services, or technology support. The key was demonstrating the mutual benefit—positive publicity for them, and tangible support for our mission. We emphasized the alignment of our values, showcasing the positive community impact that resulted from their partnership. Successful corporate partnerships significantly augmented our resources, freeing up funds to invest in vital programs.

Community outreach formed the cornerstone of our fundraising strategy. We understood that building trust and fostering relationships within our community was paramount. We organized regular health fairs, providing free health screenings, medication consultations, and health education materials. These events not only served the community but also offered valuable opportunities to engage with potential donors and volunteers. We also established partnerships with local schools and community organizations, conducting health education workshops and participating in community events. These interactions fostered a sense of mutual respect and collaboration, enhancing our visibility and building goodwill, which in turn strengthened our fundraising efforts.

Managing our resources efficiently was equally important. We implemented a rigorous budgeting and accounting system, tracking every expense meticulously. We prioritized transparency and accountability, ensuring all financial transactions were documented and accessible to stakeholders. We regularly reviewed our budget, identifying areas for cost savings and ensuring that our resources were allocated strategically to maximize their impact. To stretch every dollar further, we also embraced cost-effective strategies, negotiating favorable prices with our medication suppliers and exploring alternative sources for essential resources. This rigorous approach helped us ensure the responsible and efficient allocation of every dollar received.

Our commitment to financial sustainability extended beyond fundraising. We implemented strategies to reduce waste and optimize operations. We streamlined our administrative processes, introducing technology to handle repetitive tasks and cut down on excess paperwork. Staffing levels were reassessed to ensure just the right number of employees were in place to meet growing demands without inflating costs.

This lean approach was not about cutting corners but about maximizing the efficiency of our operations, making sure the bulk of our resources reached the patients who needed them most. We carefully scrutinized every expense, ensuring that every dollar contributed directly to our mission.

The journey was not without its challenges. Balancing our commitment to providing free or low-cost healthcare with the need for financial sustainability was a constant tightrope walk. There were times when funding fell short, forcing us to make difficult decisions and prioritize how and where to allocate our limited resources.

However, our unwavering commitment to our mission, coupled with our adaptable fundraising strategy and efficient resource management, allowed us to overcome these obstacles and continue serving our community. The success we achieved was not merely a reflection of our financial acumen but a testament to our commitment to the community, which integrated compassionate care with astute financial planning, demonstrating that even in resource-constrained environments, a sustainable and impactful healthcare initiative could thrive. It was a journey marked by perseverance, resilience, and a shared belief in the power of community.

Building a sustainable charitable pharmacy requires more than just efficient internal operations and a robust fundraising strategy;

it demands a profound commitment to collaboration and the cultivation of mutually beneficial partnerships. Our success wasn't solely a result of our internal efforts; it was inextricably linked to the broad network of allies we built within our community and beyond. This network, comprised of diverse organizations, community leaders, and dedicated volunteers, became the bedrock of our sustainability.

One of our most impactful partnerships was forged with the local medical clinic. Their doctors often referred patients to our pharmacy for medication assistance, creating a seamless referral pathway that greatly improved access to care. This collaboration wasn't simply transactional; it fostered a shared understanding of our respective roles and a mutual commitment to improving patient outcomes. Regular meetings between our pharmacy staff and the clinic's physicians allowed us to address challenges, share best practices, and ensure consistent communication, thereby preventing duplication of efforts and maximizing the impact of our combined resources.

Furthermore, the clinic provided valuable clinical insights, assisting us in refining our medication selection and ensuring the appropriateness of dispensed medications, significantly enhancing the safety and efficacy of our services. This collaborative relationship extended beyond referrals; we jointly organized health screenings and educational programs within the community to tackle broader public health issues.

Another critical partnership emerged with the local university's pharmacy school. This collaboration proved mutually advantageous. The students gained invaluable practical experience in a community pharmacy setting, working alongside our experienced staff and interacting directly with patients. This provided them with exposure to the realities of medication access challenges and the importance of patient advocacy. Conversely, the students' enthusiasm and energy injected new life into our pharmacy, helping us to adopt innovative approaches to patient care and medication management. Their participation broadened our knowledge base, introduced new technologies and best practices, and fostered an environment of continuous learning and improvement within our team. The university also provided valuable resources, including access to research databases and expert consultations, allowing us to stay informed on the latest developments in community pharmacy and medication management.

Our engagement with community leaders proved equally instrumental. We cultivated relationships with local elected officials, emphasizing the vital role our pharmacy plays in addressing the community's health needs. This led to greater understanding and support, both politically and financially.

We actively participated in local town hall meetings, providing updates on our activities and highlighting the impact of our work. This proactive communication dispelled misconceptions, secured crucial political backing for our initiatives, and even led to increased financial support from local government budgets. The relationships built with these leaders extended beyond direct funding; they provided access to critical resources and support networks and became strong voices for our mission when advocacy was needed most.

The role of volunteers in our organization cannot be overstated. We established a robust volunteer program, attracting individuals from diverse backgrounds, including retirees, students, and professionals who wanted to contribute their time and skills to our mission. Their contributions spanned a wide range of responsibilities, including medication assistance, paperwork organization, health education workshops, and outreach events. The energy and commitment they brought had a profound impact on our daily operations. We established a rigorous volunteer training program, ensuring all volunteers were properly trained and equipped to perform their tasks effectively and safely. We also implemented a system for tracking volunteer hours and recognizing their contributions, fostering a sense of ownership and commitment among our volunteers.

Beyond these specific partnerships, we prioritized the cultivation of a strong community network. We actively participated in local events, sponsoring community fairs and hosting educational workshops. This increased our visibility, promoted understanding of our mission, and facilitated broader community support. A thoughtful communication plan through newsletters, social media, and local media outlets kept supporters informed, celebrated milestones, and encouraged broader involvement. This consistent and transparent communication fostered trust and encouraged engagement from our community.

Building trust and mutual support among all stakeholders – patients, volunteers, staff, partner organizations, and funders – was paramount. This required consistent communication, transparency in our operations, and a clear articulation of our values and goals. Regular updates to our stakeholders kept them informed, fostered a sense of community, and maintained mutual understanding and support. We held regular meetings with our partner organizations, actively seeking their feedback and input to optimize our collaborative efforts. Open communication and active listening created a feedback loop, ensuring that our efforts remained relevant and impactful. Moreover, we made a concerted effort to engage our patients in the decision-making process, seeking their input on services and promoting patient empowerment.

The process of building these partnerships and fostering collaborations was not without its challenges. It took time, patience, and a willingness to work through logistical hurdles and the different ways organizations operate. However, the sustained benefits far outweighed these initial difficulties.

The network we built together became the backbone of our charitable pharmacy's long-term sustainability. It showed that when people unite with purpose and persistence, even the most complex problems faced by vulnerable communities can be addressed with lasting impact. Our experience stands as proof that meaningful collaboration can reshape healthcare for the better. The interwoven nature of these partnerships—each strengthening the other—created a resilient and effective model that continues to serve our community effectively and sustainably. The relationships, built through open dialogue, mutual respect, and a shared mission, became some of our most valuable assets. In the end, what sustained us wasn't just good financial planning. It was the deep trust and partnership within our community that made it all possible.

The success of our charitable pharmacy wasn't solely dependent on the strength of our community partnerships; it also relied heavily on our dedication to staying compliant with complex healthcare regulations. Even a charitable one requires meticulous adherence to a web of federal, state, and local regulations. Ignoring these regulations, even inadvertently, could jeopardize our operations, our reputation, and most importantly, the well-being of the patients we serve. From the outset, we recognized that regulatory compliance wasn't simply a box to be checked; it was an integral part of our operational strategy, demanding continuous vigilance and proactive adaptation.

Our journey began with a thorough assessment of all applicable regulations. This involved a detailed review of federal laws such as the Federal Food, Drug, and Cosmetic Act (FD&C Act), the Controlled Substances Act (CSA), and the Health Insurance Portability and Accountability Act (HIPAA). We also looked closely at the rules specific to our state that governed how we dispensed medications and stored them. This comprehensive analysis was critical in identifying the specific compliance requirements that directly impacted our operations.

One of the most significant regulatory hurdles we faced was maintaining proper inventory control and handling of controlled substances. The CSA imposes stringent requirements on the storage, dispensing, and record-keeping of controlled substances. To meet these standards, we set up a detailed inventory management system that included frequent physical counts, automated tracking software, and careful documentation of every transaction. We trained our staff extensively on the proper procedures for handling-controlled substances, emphasizing the importance of security, accuracy, and adherence to all applicable reporting requirements. Even the smallest discrepancy was taken seriously. We always followed up immediately, investigating the cause and putting corrective measures in place. We understood that a single lapse in this area could have severe legal and ethical consequences.

Another critical area of compliance involved patient privacy and the protection of Protected Health Information (PHI) under HIPAA. We invested in robust security measures to safeguard patient data, both electronic and paper-based.

This included implementing secure electronic health record (EHR) systems, enforcing strict access controls, and training our staff on HIPAA regulations and best practices for data privacy. We established clear protocols for handling patient information, ensuring that only authorized personnel had access to PHI and that all communications adhered to HIPAA guidelines. Regular audits and internal reviews helped us identify and address any potential vulnerabilities, minimizing the risk of data breaches and maintaining the trust of our patients.

In addition to these major areas, we addressed several other compliance needs. We ensured that our pharmacy was physically compliant with all state and local building codes and fire safety regulations. This involved regular inspections, maintenance of appropriate safety equipment, and adherence to all applicable standards. We maintained detailed records of all inspections and corrective actions, ensuring transparency and accountability. Furthermore, we remained updated on any changes in regulations through ongoing professional development for our staff and subscriptions to relevant legal and regulatory publications. We knew the rules could shift at any time, so staying informed was key to staying compliant.

Compliance wasn't simply a matter of ticking boxes; it fostered a culture of responsibility and professionalism within our organization. Our commitment to compliance extended beyond the legal requirements; it became an integral part of our mission and values. We integrated compliance into our daily operations, making it a shared responsibility among all staff members. This involved providing regular training, fostering a culture of open communication regarding compliance issues, and promoting a proactive approach to identifying and addressing potential risks. We understood that compliance wasn't just about avoiding penalties; it was about protecting our patients, upholding our ethical obligations, and building trust within our community.

A crucial aspect of our compliance strategy involved developing strong relationships with regulatory agencies. We maintained open communication with state and federal authorities, proactively seeking clarification on ambiguous regulations and fostering a collaborative relationship. This approach proved invaluable in navigating complex regulatory issues and ensuring that our interpretation and implementation of regulations were consistent with the agency's expectations.

Staying in touch regularly helped us avoid misunderstandings and made it easier to resolve any issues quickly. We viewed the regulatory agencies not as adversaries, but as partners in ensuring the safety and quality of our services.

Our compliance process was never something we set and forgot. It evolved with time and experience. We implemented a robust quality assurance (QA) program to continuously monitor and improve our compliance efforts. This involved regular internal audits, performance reviews, and staff training to address any gaps or weaknesses in our compliance systems. The QA program allowed us to identify potential risks proactively, implement corrective actions promptly, and document all improvements. This cycle of constant learning and improvement kept us on track and pushed us to do better every day.

Moreover, we incorporated technology to streamline our management systems to track controlled substances, electronic prescription management systems to ensure prescription accuracy and reduce errors, and secure electronic health record systems to protect patient privacy. These technologies helped us reduce human error, save time on routine tasks, and focus more energy on patient care. The integration of technology made our compliance efforts more efficient and less labor-intensive.

This meticulous attention to regulatory compliance, coupled with our focus on community engagement and collaborative partnerships, significantly enhanced the long-term sustainability and impact of our charitable pharmacy. It ensured the continuous provision of essential medication services to vulnerable populations, built trust with our community, and protected the reputation and integrity of our organization. Our experience demonstrated that compliance is not merely a legal obligation, but a critical component of building a sustainable and impactful community healthcare initiative. By embracing a proactive and comprehensive approach to compliance, we demonstrated our unwavering commitment to the safety, well-being, and trust of our patients and community. This commitment, we believe, is fundamental to the success of any charitable organization, particularly those operating in the highly regulated healthcare sector. The integration of compliance into our organizational culture proved to be a crucial element of our sustainability strategy, ensuring that our mission continued uninterrupted and uncompromised. The resources invested in building a strong compliance infrastructure ultimately paid dividends in terms of operational efficiency, reputational integrity, and lasting community impact.

The foundation of our charitable pharmacy's success rested on partnerships, but also on the dedication and effectiveness of our volunteer team. Creating a sustainable organization meant bringing together a team of passionate, reliable people and keeping them engaged through support and training. Recruiting the right individuals was only the first step.

Our volunteer recruitment strategy went beyond simply posting advertisements. We got involved directly with local schools, universities, and community groups. We presented our mission to potential volunteers, emphasizing the tangible impact their contribution would have on the community's health and well-being. We held informational sessions highlighting the various roles available, from assisting with prescription processing and patient counseling to administrative tasks and community outreach. We emphasized that volunteers weren't merely filling roles; they were integral members of our team, contributing to a shared mission. We also adjusted our recruitment methods to welcome people with different backgrounds and experiences, knowing that a variety of perspectives would help us better serve our diverse patient population.

The application process was designed to be straightforward and inclusive. We avoided overly complex forms, focusing instead on identifying candidates' commitment to our mission and their relevant skills and experience. We carefully reviewed applications, considering not only qualifications but also personality traits conducive to teamwork and a commitment to service. Interviews focused on understanding the applicant's motivations, expectations, and ability to work collaboratively within a team.

Once recruited, our volunteers began a well-organized and practical training journey that gave them a structured learning experience designed to equip volunteers with the knowledge and skills necessary to perform their roles effectively and safely. The training encompassed various modules, including pharmacy procedures, medication handling, patient interaction techniques, confidentiality protocols (HIPAA compliance), and conflict resolution strategies. We used a combination of classroom instruction, hands-on practice, and mentorship to ensure comprehensive understanding and competence. Experienced staff members acted as mentors, guiding volunteers and providing ongoing support and feedback.

Because our volunteers came from many different backgrounds, we knew a one-size-fits-all training wouldn't work. We adjusted our approach to fit various learning styles and skill levels. We included visual tools, interactive exercises, and role-play to make the experience more engaging and relatable. Short quizzes and checkpoints helped us keep track of how everyone was doing and figure out where extra help might be needed. We also created a training manual that included everything they'd learned, along with an online version they could access anytime for quick reference. This kept our training consistent and allowed volunteers to revisit topics at their own pace.

Retention of volunteers was as critical as recruitment. We understood that volunteers, despite their commitment, might have competing priorities or changing circumstances. To maintain engagement, we prioritized creating a positive and supportive work environment. We established regular communication channels, encouraging open feedback and addressing concerns promptly. We organized team-building activities, fostering camaraderie and a sense of shared purpose. These events ranged from informal gatherings to volunteer appreciation luncheons and participation in community events.

To show how much we valued their work, we created a thoughtful volunteer recognition program to acknowledge and appreciate the contributions of our volunteers. This wasn't merely about handing out certificates; it was about genuinely expressing gratitude and acknowledging the impact their efforts had on our organization and the community. We showcased volunteer achievements through newsletters, social media, and annual reports, emphasizing their valuable contributions. Individual recognition, such as handwritten thank-you notes, personal emails, and highlighting specific accomplishments during team meetings, created a culture of appreciation and fostered a sense of belonging. This program also ensured continuous motivation among volunteers, recognizing their efforts and strengthening their commitment to the pharmacy.

Effective communication was paramount. We established clear communication channels, using a combination of regular meetings, email updates, and a dedicated volunteer communication platform to disseminate information and address concerns. We encouraged open feedback, providing opportunities for volunteers to share their ideas and suggestions, creating a sense of ownership and involvement. Regular team meetings provided a platform for discussing challenges, sharing successes, and celebrating achievements. These meetings served not only as informational sessions but also as opportunities for team bonding and relationship building.

Resolving conflict was an important part of how we built a strong team. We provided training on conflict resolution techniques, empowering volunteers to handle disagreements in a constructive and respectful way. We emphasized the importance of active listening, empathy, and working toward solutions that everyone could accept. A clear conflict resolution protocol was established and shared with all volunteers to ensure consistent approaches to resolving any conflicts that might arise.

We also focused on empowering our volunteers, providing them with the autonomy and responsibility to contribute meaningfully to our mission. This meant assigning roles that fit their strengths and interests, helping them grow their skills while giving them a real sense of purpose. By entrusting volunteers with responsibility, we demonstrated trust and respect, thereby fostering greater engagement and commitment. We regularly sought volunteer feedback on processes and procedures, recognizing that their on-the-ground perspectives offered invaluable insights for improving efficiency and effectiveness.

The success of our volunteer management program was directly linked to our ability to adapt and evolve. We regularly reviewed and revised our recruitment, training, and retention strategies based on feedback from volunteers, staff, and external stakeholders. We continuously assessed our program's effectiveness, identifying areas for improvement and adapting our approaches to meet evolving needs. This dynamic approach ensured that our volunteer program remained relevant, engaging, and responsive to the changing needs of both our organization and the community we served.

More than just improving pharmacy operations, our investment in volunteer management had a positive ripple effect across the community. By providing opportunities for service and engagement, we fostered a sense of community ownership and responsibility. Our volunteers became advocates for our mission, extending our reach and promoting our services within their own networks. The skills and experiences gained by our volunteers were invaluable, strengthening their personal and professional development while enriching their lives. In this way, our approach to volunteer management supported not only our organization's sustainability but also the long-term health of the community itself. This commitment, we believe, is fundamental to the success of any charitable organization that seeks to create a lasting impact.

Scaling our charitable pharmacy wasn't simply about increasing the number of prescriptions filled; it was about strategically expanding our reach and impact to serve an even wider segment of the underserved population. This required careful planning, a phased approach, and a commitment to continuous improvement. Our initial focus was on enhancing our operational capacity to meet the growing demand for our services. We began with a full review of our operations, pinpointing bottlenecks and identifying areas to improve.

We began by analyzing our prescription processing workflow, identifying inefficiencies, and streamlining processes wherever possible. This included optimizing our inventory management system to minimize waste and ensure the timely restocking of essential medications. We invested in updated technology, including a new pharmacy management system that automated many tasks, freeing up our staff and volunteers to focus on patient care and community outreach. The new system also allowed for better data tracking and analysis, enabling us to monitor key metrics such as prescription fill rates, wait times, and patient satisfaction. This data-driven approach informed our decision-making, allowing us to make targeted improvements and optimize resource allocation.

Increasing our physical space was another critical step in scaling our operations. Initially, we operated in a relatively small facility, limiting our capacity to serve more patients. We explored several options, including leasing additional space within the same building or relocating to a larger facility. The decision hinged on factors such as cost, accessibility, and proximity to our target patient population. Thorough due diligence, including a cost-benefit analysis and community needs assessment, informed our choice. We ultimately secured a larger space that allowed for increased prescription filling capacity, expanded patient waiting areas, and dedicated space for health education programs and community outreach initiatives.

As our services grew, so did our need for a stronger team. While our volunteer program remained a cornerstone of our organization, we recognized the need for additional paid staff with specialized expertise. We identified key roles that needed professional expertise, including a full-time pharmacist to oversee medication safety and compliance, and an administrative assistant to handle scheduling, billing, and paperwork. Recruiting qualified professionals required a competitive compensation and benefits package, tailored to attract experienced individuals committed to our mission. We emphasized our commitment to fostering a positive work environment and providing professional development opportunities. We conducted thorough interviews, focusing not only on technical skills and experience but also on the candidate's values and alignment with our organization's mission.

Our expansion also required a more robust financial management system. We developed a detailed financial plan outlining projected expenses, revenue streams, and funding needs. This plan included strategies for diversifying our funding sources, including grants, donations, and fundraising initiatives. We developed a comprehensive fundraising strategy, including cultivating relationships with potential donors, organizing fundraising events, and creating compelling marketing materials highlighting our impact on the community. We prioritized financial transparency, ensuring donors and stakeholders felt confident and informed.

Reaching more underserved communities required a layered and intentional approach. We initiated a community needs assessment to identify areas with limited access to affordable medications. This involved collaborating with local health organizations and community leaders to understand the specific health needs of the communities we sought to serve. Based on those findings, we developed outreach programs tailored to the unique challenges of each community. This included establishing partnerships with local clinics and community centers to provide convenient access to our services and offering multilingual services to address language barriers.

We also initiated mobile pharmacy programs, utilizing a specially equipped vehicle to deliver services to remote or underserved areas. These mobile units offered basic medication dispensing, health screenings, and health education sessions, extending our reach to those who had difficulty accessing our main facility.

Technology played a pivotal role in our expansion strategy. Beyond updating our pharmacy management system, we implemented a telehealth platform to expand access to patient care. This enabled us to conduct virtual consultations with patients, providing medication management advice and addressing their concerns remotely. We also developed a user-friendly website and social media presence to improve communication and facilitate access to information about our services. This digital shift improved accessibility, especially for people with mobility challenges or those living far from our physical locations. We focused on making sure the website and platforms were simple to use, with clear information and intuitive navigation.

Sustaining our growth required a commitment to continuous improvement. We implemented a system of regular performance monitoring and evaluation, identifying areas for enhancement in our operational efficiency, patient care, and community outreach initiatives. We actively sought feedback from our patients, volunteers, and staff, incorporating their insights to refine our strategies and ensure the quality of our services. Regular staff meetings allowed us to address challenges proactively and celebrate successes collaboratively. We maintained open communication channels, ensuring transparency and fostering a sense of shared ownership among our team.

Looking ahead, we plan to establish satellite pharmacies in carefully chosen areas to improve service access in high-need regions. We are exploring partnerships with other community-based organizations to expand our collaborative efforts, leveraging resources and expertise to reach a wider range of individuals and families.

We plan to introduce specialized programs to address specific health needs within the community, such as diabetes management and chronic disease care. This might include collaborations with healthcare professionals to offer workshops and counseling sessions on topics relevant to the target community.

Our volunteer program continues to evolve, with expanded training opportunities and more ways for people to get involved. We also plan to invest in professional development opportunities for our staff to enhance their skills and knowledge, ensuring we remain at the forefront of pharmacy best practices and patient care. We will continue our commitment to data-driven decision-making, using performance metrics to evaluate the effectiveness of our programs and make informed adjustments to our strategies. Our mission is to keep expanding thoughtfully, never losing sight of our promise to provide compassionate, affordable care. This requires a continuous cycle of assessment, refinement, and innovation – a never-ending pursuit of excellence in fulfilling our community's healthcare needs. The core of our work remains providing essential medication and compassionate care; however, scaling operations requires a strategic and thoughtful approach. Growth without strategy is simply expansion without impact, and our commitment to both underscores our mission's long-term success.

Chapter 12: Measuring Success and Impact

The success of our charitable pharmacy isn't measured solely by numbers; it's reflected in the lives we touch. The faces of our patients, their stories of relief and renewed hope, are the truest testament to our mission. Behind every prescription filled, every consultation offered, lies a personal narrative of struggle overcome, health restored, and dignity preserved.

These are not just statistics; they are the heart of our work.

Mrs. Rodriguez, a diabetic grandmother of five, had been rationing her insulin for months due to the escalating cost of her medication. The strain was evident in her weary eyes and the tremor in her hands. She had been forced to choose between her medication and groceries, a choice no one should ever have to make. Her story, shared with us in halting English punctuated by tears, is unfortunately all too common. Upon discovering our pharmacy, Mrs. Rodriguez found not only affordable insulin but also a supportive community. Our pharmacists provided her with comprehensive diabetes education, counseling her on lifestyle changes and medication management. Her subsequent visits revealed a remarkable transformation. The weariness in her eyes was replaced by a spark of hope, her tremor subsided, and her overall health improved significantly. She now attends our diabetes support group, actively participating and offering encouragement to fellow patients.

Her journey illustrates the life-changing impact that access to affordable healthcare can have on an individual's well-being and quality of life.

Mr. Jones, a retired construction worker, suffered a debilitating stroke that left him with limited mobility and a dependence on several prescription medications. His fixed income barely covered his rent, leaving him with little to spare for his medical needs. He initially felt ashamed to seek assistance, burdened by a lifetime of independence and self-reliance. However, our outreach programs reached him, gently breaking down the barriers to care. We provided not only his essential medications at significantly reduced costs but also facilitated transportation to his appointments, helping him navigate the often-complex healthcare system. His transformation has been gradual, marked by a slow but steady regain of his dignity and independence. He now volunteers at our pharmacy, his infectious enthusiasm and unwavering spirit inspiring both patients and staff alike. His presence serves as a constant reminder of the ripple effect of compassion and support.

Then there's young Sarah, a bright-eyed college student struggling to balance her studies with the high cost of her asthma medication. Asthma attacks frequently interrupted her classes, jeopardizing her academic progress and causing her significant anxiety. Our pharmacy offered her a lifeline, providing her with affordable medication and access to a pharmacist who patiently answered her questions and addressed her concerns. The reduction in her medical expenses allowed her to focus on her studies, resulting in improved academic performance and a renewed sense of hope for her future. Her story exemplifies the importance of affordable healthcare in enabling individuals to pursue their educational and career goals, contributing meaningfully to society.

These are but a few of the countless stories that paint a vivid picture of our impact. Behind every name and every face is a journey of resilience, a testament to the human spirit's ability to overcome adversity. Their experiences underscore the crucial role that accessible and affordable healthcare plays in fostering thriving communities. We are humbled by their trust and inspired by their strength.

The impact extends beyond the individual to their families and their communities. When a parent can afford their child's medication, it eliminates the stress and worry that often accompany financial hardship. When a grandparent can manage their chronic illness, they can remain actively involved in their family's lives, offering their love, support, and wisdom. When community members have access to affordable healthcare, they are better equipped to contribute to the social and economic vitality of their neighborhoods.

We carefully document each patient interaction, collecting data not only on medication dispensing but also on patient satisfaction, medication adherence, and overall health outcomes. This comprehensive approach allows us to evaluate the effectiveness of our programs and identify areas for improvement.

The consistent, positive feedback we receive from our patients, combined with measurable improvements in their health indicators, confirms the meaningful impact of our efforts.

We've received numerous heartfelt testimonials emphasizing the profound effect our pharmacy has had on patients' lives. One patient described our pharmacy as "a beacon of hope in a sea of despair," while another expressed gratitude for the "compassionate care that extends far beyond just filling prescriptions." These testimonials reflect the dedication of our staff and volunteers, who strive to provide not only excellent service but a genuine human connection.

Beyond individual stories, our data reveals significant improvements in key health metrics. We have seen a dramatic decrease in emergency room visits and hospitalizations among our patients, suggesting improved management of chronic conditions. Medication adherence rates have significantly increased, leading to better disease control and overall health outcomes. These tangible results demonstrate that affordable access to healthcare translates to improved health outcomes for our community.

We have actively solicited feedback from our patients, using various methods such as surveys, focus groups, and informal conversations. These feedback sessions have revealed recurring themes, underscoring the value of our integrated approach. Patients consistently express appreciation for the personal touch, the empathetic counseling, and the sense of community they find within our pharmacy. Many describe feeling heard and understood, a crucial aspect of healthcare that often gets overlooked in traditional settings.

The future growth of our charitable pharmacy will continue to be guided by the invaluable feedback and inspiring stories shared by our patients, strengthening our resolve to improve the health and well-being of our community. These narratives remain the heart of our work, and we remain committed to providing essential care and fostering a sense of belonging and hope for every individual we serve.

Quantifying the impact of our charitable pharmacy requires a multifaceted approach, moving beyond anecdotal evidence to encompass a robust system of data collection and analysis.

While the individual stories of Mrs. Rodriguez, Mr. Jones, and Sarah powerfully illustrate the human element of our work, a comprehensive understanding of our success necessitates a rigorous examination of quantifiable metrics. This allows us to not only demonstrate our effectiveness to funders and stakeholders but also to continuously improve our programs and better serve our community.

Our data collection strategy is designed to capture a holistic view of our impact, extending beyond simply the number of prescriptions dispensed. We meticulously track several key performance indicators (KPIs), enabling us to assess various aspects of our operation and its effectiveness in addressing healthcare disparities. These KPIs fall into several broad categories: patient demographics, medication dispensing data, patient satisfaction, health outcome measures, and cost savings.

Firstly, we meticulously document patient demographics, including age, gender, income level, insurance status, and primary diagnosis. This detailed information allows us to identify specific populations most in need of our services and tailor our outreach programs accordingly. For example, our data revealed a disproportionately high number of elderly patients with uncontrolled hypertension, prompting us to include medication provision, lifestyle counseling, and regular blood pressure monitoring. This targeted approach has demonstrably improved patient adherence to prescribed medications, leading to a significant reduction in hypertension-related complications. The program's success was evident in the decrease in hospital admissions for hypertensive emergencies and a notable drop in average systolic blood pressure among enrolled patients. This measurable improvement showcased the effectiveness of our tailored approach and underscored the importance of data-driven program design.

Secondly, our medication dispensing data provides a crucial measure of our operational efficiency and reach. We track the number of prescriptions filled per month, the types of medications dispensed most frequently, and the average cost per prescription. This information helps us optimize our inventory management, anticipate fluctuations in demand, and negotiate better prices with pharmaceutical suppliers.

For instance, we noticed a consistently high demand for insulin among our diabetic patients. Through strategic negotiations with manufacturers and wholesalers, we managed to secure significant discounts on insulin, ensuring affordability for our most vulnerable patients. This illustrates how data-driven purchasing contributes to increased access and reduces the financial burden on patients. We carefully analyze this data not just for operational efficiency but also to better understand the prevalent health conditions within our community, allowing for more targeted and proactive health interventions.

Beyond sheer numbers, we prioritize patient satisfaction. Regular surveys, feedback forms, and informal conversations with patients provide invaluable insights into their experiences with our pharmacy. These assessments are critical, as they offer a direct measure of patient perception and help us identify areas for improvement. For example, patient feedback revealed a need for improved communication regarding medication side effects and interactions. As a response, we revamped our patient education materials and introduced one-on-one counseling sessions to address these concerns more effectively. By implementing these changes, we saw a significant decrease in medication-related adverse events and a marked improvement in patient satisfaction scores. The results of patient satisfaction surveys are analyzed and reported regularly, providing crucial feedback for continuous improvement and enabling us to constantly enhance the overall patient experience.

The impact of our pharmacy extends beyond improved patient satisfaction to tangible improvements in health outcomes. We monitor various health metrics such as blood pressure, blood glucose levels, and cholesterol levels, particularly for patients with chronic conditions. Tracking these metrics over time allows us to objectively assess the effectiveness of our medication dispensing and health counseling programs. For instance, our data showed a significant reduction in average blood glucose levels among diabetic patients following their participation in our diabetes education and management program, further demonstrating the positive outcomes of our intervention. Furthermore, we've noticed a decrease in emergency room visits related to asthma exacerbations due to our targeted medication dispensing and patient education on proper inhaler use, validating our efforts. Regular monitoring and evaluation of health outcomes provide critical evidence of our impact and support our efforts to secure continued funding and community support.

Finally, we meticulously track cost savings. We compare the cost of medications dispensed through our pharmacy with the retail price of the same medications, providing clear evidence of the financial relief we offer to our patients. Analyzing this data allows us to quantify the cost savings achieved per patient, per year, and for the entire community. We also consider the indirect cost savings by tracking reduced emergency room visits and hospitalizations, which translates to a significant reduction in healthcare spending at the community level. This analysis not only demonstrates the fiscal responsibility of our operation but also serves as a powerful argument for increasing access to affordable healthcare, showing a clear return on investment for community support and charitable donations.

By systematically collecting and analyzing this diverse set of data, we build a comprehensive narrative of our impact. Our findings are not just numbers on a spreadsheet; they translate into real-world improvements in the health and well-being of our community. This quantifiable evidence serves as a cornerstone of our ongoing efforts, driving our strategic planning, guiding our resource allocation, and fueling our passion for expanding our reach and influence within the community. It empowers us to demonstrate our value, attract further support, and continue our critical mission of providing accessible and affordable healthcare to those who need it most. This commitment to data-driven decision-making ensures that our efforts are not only compassionate but also strategically effective in addressing healthcare disparities.

The combination of powerful individual stories and quantifiable data paints a complete picture of our work, illustrating the genuine, transformative impact of our charitable pharmacy.

One significant social determinant we address is access to medication. For many of our patients, the financial burden of prescription drugs is insurmountable. The cost of essential medications can quickly deplete household budgets, leading to difficult choices between food, housing, and healthcare.

Our pharmacy removes this barrier, ensuring patients receive the medications they need to manage chronic conditions and avoid preventable hospitalizations.

This directly translates into improved financial stability for families, allowing them to focus on other essential needs rather than worrying about constantly rising pharmaceutical costs. We've witnessed firsthand how this improved financial security leads to decreased stress levels and a general improvement in overall well-being within families. Anecdotal evidence from patient interviews highlights the relief experienced by caregivers who no longer have to make impossible choices regarding essential medications for their loved ones. The weight lifted from their shoulders allows them to better care for themselves and their families, creating a positive ripple effect throughout the community.

Beyond financial stability, our pharmacy fosters a sense of community and social support.

The waiting area often transforms into an informal hub where patients connect, share stories, and offer each other encouragement. This sense of belonging and shared experience is invaluable, particularly for those facing chronic illnesses or social isolation. Many of our patients feel atmosphere we cultivate strengthens community bonds and reduces the feeling of isolation often associated with chronic health conditions. We've seen instances where patients have become friends, supporting each other outside the walls of the pharmacy. These social connections are a crucial component of overall health and well-being, significantly enhancing their quality of life. The pharmacy isn't just a place to obtain medication; it becomes a beacon of hope and a source of valuable social interaction, building resilience within the community.

Furthermore, improved health outcomes achieved through our services contribute to a more productive workforce. By helping patients effectively manage chronic conditions, we reduce workplace absenteeism and increase productivity. Individuals with better control of their health are better equipped to participate fully in the workforce, contributing to the economic vitality of our community. The economic implications extend beyond individual productivity, as a healthier workforce contributes to a stronger local economy. We've collaborated with local businesses to offer wellness programs, integrating our services with workplace initiatives to improve employee health and reduce lost productivity. This collaborative approach demonstrates the far-reaching impact of accessible healthcare and fosters a healthier, more engaged workforce.

Our commitment to addressing social determinants of health extends to promoting healthy lifestyles. We've incorporated health education into our services, offering counseling on nutrition, exercise, and preventative care. This holistic approach recognizes that medication alone is insufficient for optimal health. We actively collaborate with local community organizations, offering joint workshops on healthy eating habits, stress management techniques, and physical activity. The collaborative partnerships expand our reach and allow us to impact broader community health. For example, a joint initiative with the local YMCA provided subsidized memberships to our patients, facilitating access to exercise facilities and fostering healthier lifestyles. The success of this initiative was tracked by monitoring participant attendance and reported self-improvement in health behaviors. These joint programs strengthen the community's health infrastructure and contribute to a healthier and more resilient population.

Our impact on education is also noteworthy. We offer educational materials and workshops on medication management, emphasizing the importance of adherence and proper usage. These resources empower patients to take an active role in their healthcare, building knowledge and confidence. We've developed tailored programs for specific conditions, such as diabetes and hypertension, which incorporate education and support systems for improved self-care. These educational initiatives empower our patients to actively engage in their healthcare journey, reducing healthcare costs and promoting independent self-care practices. For example, our diabetes management program reduced hospitalizations due to uncontrolled blood sugar levels. These reduced hospitalizations lead to not only improved patient health but also a reduction in the community's overall healthcare burden.

The data we collect allows us to showcase this community's impact. We demonstrate how improved medication access reduces emergency room visits and hospitalizations, resulting in significant cost savings for the healthcare system and our community. This cost-effectiveness argument strengthens our position when seeking funding or partnerships. By meticulously tracking these health outcomes, we can quantify our advocacy efforts, enabling us to demonstrate the value of our work and its effectiveness in improving overall community well-being.

Furthermore, we actively engage in community partnerships, collaborating with local healthcare providers, social service agencies, and other organizations. These partnerships extend our reach and allow us to offer a more comprehensive model of care. We participate in local health fairs, providing screenings, educational materials, and medication consultations. These collaborative ventures amplify our message and broaden the community's access to healthcare services. This collaborative approach builds a stronger network of support for our community's most vulnerable populations, strengthening community resilience and fostering a sense of shared responsibility for health and well-being. Our collaborations have expanded to include school health programs, providing necessary medication and education to students with chronic health conditions. This joint effort improves students' health and allows them to focus on their education, supporting the community's development.

In conclusion, the impact of our charitable pharmacy transcends the individual level, profoundly shaping the health and well-being of the entire community. By addressing social determinants of health and promoting a holistic approach to care, we contribute to a more equitable, healthier, and prosperous community. Our data-driven approach allows us not only to demonstrate our success but to continuously improve our services, ensuring that our efforts effectively serve the diverse needs of the population we serve. This ongoing dedication to community service and health equity forms the core of our mission and fuels our passion for expanding our reach and creating lasting, positive change in our community.

The sustainability of our charitable pharmacy is inextricably linked to the community's well-being, a symbiotic relationship that demands careful planning and proactive strategies. Our long-term vision transcends simply filling prescriptions; it envisions a future where healthcare access is no longer a barrier to a thriving community. This requires a multifaceted approach, addressing financial stability, organizational strength, and a steadfast commitment to our core mission.

Securing consistent funding is paramount. Our current model relies on a diverse portfolio of income streams, including grants, individual donations, corporate sponsorships, and fundraising events. However, reliance on short-term grants is inherently precarious. To mitigate this risk, we are actively developing a comprehensive fundraising strategy that diversifies our funding sources and ensures long-term financial security. This includes cultivating relationships with major philanthropic organizations, establishing an endowment fund, and exploring innovative fundraising initiatives. For example, we are pursuing partnerships with local businesses to co-create branded products, with a portion of proceeds supporting our pharmacy.

Strengthening our organizational structure is equally crucial. We are committed to building a robust governance model, recruiting a skilled and dedicated board of directors, and establishing clear lines of accountability and responsibility.

Professional development opportunities for our staff are essential to ensure we maintain a highly competent and motivated team. This includes providing opportunities for continuing education, leadership training, and mentorship programs. We recognize that our staff are the cornerstone of our success, and investing in their development is an investment in the future of the pharmacy. This dedication also extends to fostering a strong and positive work environment, promoting a culture of collaboration and mutual support. We believe that a happy and motivated team is better equipped to serve our community effectively.

Maintaining a clear and compelling mission statement that resonates with both our stakeholders and the wider community is vital. Regular evaluation of our strategic plan, ensuring it remains relevant and responsive to the evolving needs of the community, is a crucial aspect of our long-term sustainability. We engage in continuous monitoring and evaluation of our programs and services, using data-driven insights to inform decision-making and refine our approaches. This ongoing assessment includes feedback from patients, staff, and community partners, enabling us to identify areas for improvement and adapt to changing circumstances. We believe that continuous improvement and a commitment to data-driven decision-making are crucial for ensuring the long-term viability and effectiveness of our charitable pharmacy.

Looking ahead, several key strategies are integral to our long-term vision. We plan to expand our service offerings to address unmet healthcare needs within the community. This might involve incorporating new programs such as mental health support, substance abuse counseling, or chronic disease management programs. The expansion will also involve strengthening our partnerships with local healthcare providers, social service organizations, and schools. Such collaborations enable us to offer a more holistic and comprehensive approach to community health. We aim to build a strong network of support that helps us reach more individuals and families who may need our services. We are also exploring the possibility of establishing satellite clinics in underserved areas to bring our services closer to those who need them most. This expansion is driven by our commitment to ensure equitable access to care for all members of our community.

Technological advancements are also integral to our future. We are exploring the use of telehealth services to provide remote consultations and medication management, particularly beneficial for patients with mobility challenges or those residing in remote areas. This initiative aims to bridge geographic barriers and improve access to care. In addition, we are investing in electronic health record systems to enhance efficiency, improve data management, and ensure patient privacy and security. Technology will allow us to streamline our operations, improve patient care coordination, and allow for better data analysis to measure the impact of our programs. Furthermore, we will continue to invest in data analytics to track our progress, identify areas for improvement, and demonstrate the value of our services to potential funders and stakeholders.

Community engagement will remain a core element of our operational model. We plan to continue participating in community events, health fairs, and educational workshops to raise awareness of our services and promote healthy lifestyles. These outreach initiatives will involve partnerships with schools, community centers, churches, and local businesses. Through active engagement with the community, we will strengthen our relationships, fostering a spirit of collaboration and shared responsibility for community health. We also intend to involve community members in the decision-making process, ensuring our programs remain relevant and responsive to their needs. This community-centered approach is crucial for building trust and establishing strong partnerships, ensuring our sustainability and effectiveness.

Financial planning for the long term includes diversifying funding sources to minimize reliance on any single stream of income. We will actively pursue grants from various foundations, solicit individual donations through direct mail campaigns and online platforms, and develop corporate sponsorship programs. We will also establish a comprehensive endowment fund to provide a stable source of long-term funding. The endowment will serve as a financial cushion, offering protection against fluctuations in other funding streams. Our sustainable financial model will also explore partnerships with government agencies and private sector organizations, identifying opportunities for joint funding and collaborative efforts to expand our service reach.

Transparency and accountability are integral to building trust with our stakeholders. We will continue to publish annual reports detailing our financial performance, operational activities, and community impact. These reports will be accessible to the public and will provide clear and concise information about our work. Regular audits will be conducted to ensure financial integrity and responsible stewardship of resources. Open communication and regular reporting will allow stakeholders to understand the workings of the pharmacy, its challenges, and its impact on the community.

This will not only strengthen our financial position but also build credibility and reinforce the trust our community has in our work.

Our long-term vision extends beyond simply providing medication; it encompasses fostering a healthier and more equitable community. We will continuously strive to adapt and evolve, remaining responsive to the changing needs of the population we serve. We recognize that the success of our efforts is closely tied to the overall health and well-being of the community, and this mutual relationship will inform all our future plans. Our ongoing commitment to community service, paired with a robust and sustainable operational structure, ensures that our charitable pharmacy will continue to make a significant and lasting impact on the lives of those we serve for years to come. The ultimate measure of our impact we have made on the overall health and well-being of the community. By continuously evaluating our programs, embracing innovation, and fostering strong community partnerships, we will ensure that our charitable pharmacy remains a vital resource for generations to come.

Reflecting on the journey of establishing and maintaining our charitable pharmacy, several key lessons stand out. Firstly, the importance of community engagement cannot be overstated. Building trust and fostering strong relationships with community members, healthcare providers, and local businesses was instrumental in our success. This wasn't merely a matter of public relations; it was about actively listening to the community's needs, incorporating their feedback into our programs, and ensuring our services were truly relevant and accessible. We learned that simply providing medication wasn't enough; we needed to understand the broader social determinants of health affecting our patients and address them holistically. This understanding led to the development of partnerships with social service organizations, enabling referrals for housing assistance, food banks, and other critical support services. This holistic approach proved to be far more impactful than simply dispensing prescriptions.

Secondly, the significance of financial diversification became acutely apparent. While initial funding from grants and individual donations was crucial, we discovered the inherent instability of relying heavily on short-term funding cycles.

This realization prompted us to develop a robust and sustainable financial model. This included establishing an endowment fund, securing corporate sponsorships, and cultivating long-term relationships with philanthropic organizations. This process taught us the importance of financial planning, budgeting, and resource management, skills that are essential for any sustainable organization. We learned to build strong cases for funding, highlighting not just our operational needs but also our demonstrable community impact. We found that showcasing concrete results – improved patient outcomes, increased medication adherence, and enhanced community health indicators – was essential in attracting and retaining funding.

Thirdly, the value of data-driven decision-making proved invaluable. From the outset, we recognized the need for rigorous data collection and analysis to track our progress and measure our impact. This involved implementing electronic health record systems, creating robust data management protocols, and engaging in ongoing program evaluation. The data allowed us to identify areas of strength and weakness, refine our strategies, and make informed decisions based on evidence. It also allowed us to demonstrate the effectiveness of our programs to potential funders and stakeholders, strengthening our case for continued support. This continuous improvement cycle – gathering data, analyzing results, adapting our approach, and measuring impact – was key to our sustainability.

Looking towards the future, we have ambitious plans to further expand our reach and impact. One primary goal is to increase access to care for underserved populations within our community. This will involve exploring the establishment of satellite clinics in areas with limited healthcare access.

These satellite locations will offer a range of services, including prescription medication dispensing, basic health screenings, and health education programs. To ensure the success of these satellite clinics, we will need to secure additional funding, recruit and train staff, and develop effective strategies for outreach and community engagement. We will apply the lessons learned from our main facility to create flexible, scalable models for these new locations, maximizing their effectiveness while minimizing financial risk.

Another key area of future development is the expansion of our services to address unmet healthcare needs. We are exploring the integration of additional services such as mental health support, substance abuse counseling, and chronic disease management programs. These services will require collaboration with healthcare professionals, mental health specialists, and community organizations. This approach is based on our understanding that health is not just about the absence of disease, but rather a state of complete physical, mental, and social well-being. By addressing the multifaceted needs of our community, we aim to achieve a more meaningful and lasting impact. We believe that integrating these crucial services directly into our model will create a more streamlined and accessible system for patients, reducing barriers to comprehensive care.

Technology will play a vital role in our future expansion plans. We plan to invest in advanced telehealth technologies to provide remote consultations and medication management to patients in remote areas or those with mobility limitations.

This will improve access to care, particularly for individuals who face significant barriers in accessing traditional healthcare settings. We will also continue to upgrade our electronic health record systems to enhance data security, improve patient privacy, and streamline our operational processes. Investing in efficient technology will enable us to focus more resources on patient care and community engagement. We will explore the use of data analytics to gain deeper insights into patient needs, track health outcomes, and demonstrate our impact to stakeholders. By employing the power of technology responsibly, we can further enhance our capacity to serve the community effectively and efficiently.

Transparency and accountability will remain integral to our operations. We will continue to publish annual reports detailing our financial performance, operational activities, and community impact. These reports will be readily available to the public and will demonstrate our responsible stewardship of resources. We believe that transparency builds trust with our stakeholders and strengthens our credibility within the community. We will conduct regular audits to ensure our financial integrity and to provide assurance to our funders and partners. We will actively seek feedback from patients, staff, and community members to identify areas for improvement and guide our future direction. This commitment to openness will enhance our ability to adapt to the ever-evolving needs of the community.

Building and sustaining a charitable pharmacy is a continuous journey of learning, adaptation, and commitment. Throughout this process, we've recognized the importance of community engagement, financial diversification, data-driven decision-making, and ongoing evaluation for improvement. Looking ahead, our plans include strategic expansion, integration of new services, and the use of technology to broaden our reach and impact. Transparency and accountability will continue to be the cornerstones of the trust we share with our stakeholders. In the end, our success won't be measured by financial metrics alone, but by the lasting impact we make on the health and well-being of the communities we serve. This mutual relationship—a thriving community nurturing a thriving pharmacy—is the vision we're dedicated to fulfilling.

Chapter 13: Prescriptions of Hope

It was a busy afternoon at the pharmacy when a young waitress, referred by St. Peter's Charity Clinic, walked in looking anxious and exhausted. She explained that she was pregnant, had diabetes, and was just barely over the Medicaid income limit, making her ineligible for coverage. The cost of her insulin was $800 a month, far beyond what she and her husband could afford, but essential to keep both her and her unborn baby healthy.

We assured her that at the Ritesh Shah Charitable Pharmacy, we would provide her insulin at no cost, so she wouldn't have to choose between her health and her baby's future. Each month, she returned quietly, full of gratitude and hope, as we handed her the medication that would carry her safely through her pregnancy.

Nine months later, her husband came into the pharmacy, his face lit with joy. He held out his phone and proudly showed us a photo of their healthy newborn. With tears in his eyes, he said, "If it was not for Señor Ritesh, this could have been so different for us. You made this possible."

One of our board members, witnessing the moment, smiled and asked, "So, did you name the baby Ritesh?" The couple laughed, and the pharmacy was filled with warmth and gratitude.

Moments like these remind us that every prescription is more than just medicine. It is hope, it is life, and it is the reason we do what we do. This is Pills to Purpose in action, happening right at our counter, changing lives one patient and one family at a time.

The pharmacy staff, including Program Director Ayan, reacted with heartfelt joy and emotion when the husband shared the picture and his gratitude. Seeing the baby and hearing the father's words served as a powerful reminder of why we do this work. The atmosphere was full of warmth and laughter, especially when the joke about the baby's name brought everyone closer together.

Encounters like this not only lift the team's spirits but also deepen their commitment to serving families. These shared moments create bonds and bring renewed meaning to the work we do every day.

When the husband described how receiving insulin through the pharmacy helped them survive those difficult months, the entire staff was moved. As first-time parents, they were able to focus on welcoming their child into the world instead of worrying about unaffordable medication.

Knowing that the savings allowed them to buy toys and a crib for their baby made the impact even more personal. These small but profound details bring purpose to our profession. They remind us that our work goes far beyond dispensing medicine—we are helping build futures, create stability, and offer peace of mind.

Shortly after CBS 2 News aired a segment about the opening of Ritesh Shah Charitable Pharmacy in Red Bank, word spread quickly through the community. One afternoon, a man walked in—his eyes full of hope, his body showing signs of fatigue. He spoke little English but held a small slip of paper with the names of his medications: Keppra 500mg, Augmentin 875mg, Meclizine 25mg, and Carbidopa-Levodopa.

Using a mix of gestures and broken words, he explained that his doctor had seen the news and told him about the pharmacy. He believed he could come here for help, even without a prescription in hand. He had walked a long distance, guided by desperation and the hope that someone might help him get the medicine he needed for his chronic conditions.

That day, I happened to be volunteering. It was clear this was not going to be a routine visit. He was hungry, so we began by offering him food and a place to rest. While he ate, our team went to work—making calls, tracking down his doctor, overcoming language barriers, and sorting out paperwork. It took time, effort, and patience, but we never considered giving up.

After what felt like hours, we finally reached his doctor and secured the necessary prescriptions. When we handed him the medications, his gratitude was overwhelming. He clasped our hands, eyes brimming with tears, and offered blessings in his language.

At that moment, the pharmacy became something more than a place to receive treatment. It became a refuge—a sanctuary where hope was restored, and dignity preserved.

Stories like his remind us why this pharmacy exists. Our

mission has never been just about filling prescriptions. It is about meeting people where they are, breaking through barriers, and offering kindness when it is needed most.

Every day, we see the difference that access—and a little compassion—can make. And every day, we are reminded that this is what turning pills into purpose truly looks like.

The pharmacy faced several challenges in providing medication to the patient who arrived after seeing the CBS 2 News story:

Lack of Prescription: The patient came without a valid prescription, presenting both regulatory and ethical challenges. Pharmacies are required by law to dispense medications only with proper documentation, and handling such requests is often complex. It took significant effort to contact his doctor, verify his medical needs, and ensure full compliance with legal requirements.

Language Barrier: The patient did not speak English, which made communication difficult. It required extra time, patience, and sensitivity from our staff to understand his condition and explain each step of the process.

Patient Poverty and Limited Access: The patient's financial hardship and lack of access to regular healthcare reflected the broader issues community pharmacies face when serving underserved populations. Many patients arrive in moments of crisis, in need of not just medicine, but also food, shelter, and emotional support.

Time and Resource Constraints: This situation required multitasking and seamless coordination. Our team had to simultaneously manage dispensing, patient care, provider communication, and immediate support—like offering food—all while continuing to assist other patients.

When the patient finally received his medication, his reaction was deeply emotional and unforgettable. He had arrived hungry, without money, and unable to communicate fluently—but full of hope. As we handed him his medications, tears streamed down his face. He wept openly, overwhelmed with relief and gratitude.

Recognizing his vulnerability, we made sure he was fed and arranged a cab to return him safely to his shelter in Asbury Park.

Moments like this demonstrate how charitable pharmacies do more than provide medication—they restore dignity, offer comfort, and empower individuals during their most difficult times.

For years, one of our patients from the Parker Clinic lived in constant anxiety, forced to ration his life-saving insulin. He had been prescribed both Humalog and Basaglar, but due to the high costs, he could only afford to take half his recommended dose. Every month, he faced the impossible decision of which of his nine other medications he could afford, knowing full well that skipping any could endanger his health.

When he first walked into the Ritesh Shah Charitable Pharmacy, his story was sadly all too familiar. He spoke candidly about the stress and fear he felt, never certain if his insulin would last until the next month. The burden of choosing between his medications and basic needs—like food or rent—had taken a serious toll on his well-being.

Studies show that when patients are forced to ration insulin due to cost, their health outcomes worsen significantly, and the risk of severe complications increases dramatically.

That all changed the day he joined our pharmacy. Through our charitable medication program, he began receiving his full supply of insulin—and all nine of his other prescriptions—at no cost. The relief was immediate. He no longer had to choose between survival and health. Instead of managing fear, he could finally manage his condition.

Research supports what we see every day: when patients receive consistent access to medications through financial assistance programs like ours, adherence improves, health outcomes stabilize, and quality of life returns.

Now, each time he picks up his medications, the room fills with a sense of calm and quiet gratitude. He tells us he sleeps better, feels more energetic, and can focus on living instead of just getting by.

Our pharmacy has become more than a place to collect medicine—it is a source of stability and reassurance for patients like him. As I reflect on his journey, I am reminded of the promise I made to my sister—to serve others in her memory. I know she would be proud to see the lives we are helping to transform: patients receiving the care they deserve, and families spared the pain of preventable loss.

This is the true purpose behind every prescription we fill: saving lives, restoring dignity, and delivering hope where it is needed most.

After receiving support from the charitable pharmacy, the patient's life changed dramatically. No longer forced to ration insulin or skip medications, he was finally able to access everything he needed, without financial strain. That consistency brought him not only better health but a renewed sense of peace and stability. For the first time in years, he could focus on healing rather than struggling—and that, to us, is the essence of care.

Research shows that patients who use charitable pharmacies report significant improvements in their overall health, a better understanding of their medications, and a stronger sense of control over their own well-being. In this patient's case, regular access to medication meant fewer health crises and a reduced risk of complications, as well as less reliance on emergency care.

Emotionally, the relief of not having to choose between medicine and other basic needs lifted a huge burden.

Patients like him often express deep gratitude, and their renewed hope and trust in the healthcare system can lead to better adherence and improved outcomes.

Ultimately, the charitable pharmacy did more than just provide medication-it restored dignity, empowered the patient to manage his health, and helped save lives by closing the gap for those who fall through the cracks of traditional coverage.

After receiving assistance from the Ritesh Shah Charitable Pharmacy, the patient's experience transformed in several meaningful ways:

Consistent Medication Access: He no longer had to ration insulin or decide which prescriptions to skip each month. The pharmacy provided a steady, ongoing supply of insulin and other essential medications, removing the stress and danger of inconsistent use.

Improved Health and Peace of Mind: With uninterrupted access to all his medications, the patient experienced fewer complications and was able to focus on maintaining his health instead of worrying about whether he could afford his next dose. This stability brought him peace of mind and a renewed sense of safety.

Restored Dignity and Empowerment: The pharmacy's patient-centered approach—grounded in dignity and respect—helped him feel seen, supported, and capable of managing his health. He remained with his family, continued working, and began to live his life with new hope and confidence.

Reduced Financial Burden: By eliminating the cost barrier to vital medications, the pharmacy freed up limited resources for other essentials, reducing the risk of having to choose between food, rent, and health.

Broader Community Impact: His story reflects a larger pattern among communities served by charitable pharmacies—improved health outcomes, fewer hospital visits, and stronger trust in the healthcare system among vulnerable populations.

In summary, the charitable pharmacy did much more than dispense medicine; it changed the patient's outlook, restored his dignity, and helped save his life by closing critical gaps in access and care.

During January and February of 2022, the groundwork for the Ritesh Shah Charitable Pharmacy was laid through a series of meaningful meetings with key community partners.

Recognizing that no single organization could tackle healthcare disparities alone, I reached out to leaders at Parker Family Health Center, Pilgrim Baptist Church, and Lunch Break. These organizations were already deeply embedded in the community, serving vulnerable populations with food, shelter, and primary care. Our shared goal was clear: to form lasting relationships that would help bridge gaps in medication access for uninsured and underserved patients.

Each meeting was more than just a business discussion—it was a gathering of like-minded individuals united by a sense of mission. Over lunch, we exchanged stories about patients who had fallen through the cracks of the healthcare system, and we brainstormed ways to ensure that no one would have to choose between medicine and other basic needs. These conversations were candid and heartfelt, fueled by a mutual understanding that health is a fundamental right, not a privilege. We discussed logistics, eligibility criteria, and how best to refer patients between our organizations, always keeping the focus on reducing health inequities in our community.

The partnership with Parker Clinic was especially significant. As a trusted provider of free and low-cost healthcare, Parker Clinic became a vital referral source for patients who needed medications but couldn't afford them. We coordinated workflows so that clinic staff could help patients complete eligibility forms and send prescriptions directly to the Ritesh Shah Charitable Pharmacy, ensuring a seamless process for those in need. Similarly, Pilgrim Baptist Church and Lunch Break brought their deep community ties and outreach expertise, helping us reach patients who might not otherwise know about the new pharmacy.

These early collaborations set the tone for our mission: to increase access to medications, immunizations, and health education, and to build a healthier community by addressing both clinical and social health inequities. Together, we developed a shared vision—one where every patient, regardless of income or insurance status, could receive the medications they need to live healthier lives. The trust and cooperation built during those early months became the foundation of the pharmacy's success, and these relationships continue to be a cornerstone of our work.

Looking back, those winter meetings were about more than forming partnerships—they were about building a coalition of hope. By coming together, sharing meals, and aligning our efforts, we took the first steps toward creating a safety net for our most vulnerable neighbors. This collaborative spirit remains at the heart of the Ritesh Shah Charitable Pharmacy, fueling our ongoing fight against healthcare disparities in New Jersey.

To form strong relationships with Parker Clinic, Pilgrim Baptist Church, and Lunch Break in early 2022, we implemented several specific initiatives focused on building trust, collaboration, and shared purpose:

Personal Outreach and Vision Sharing: I initiated direct meetings with leaders from each organization, clearly outlining the vision and mission of the Ritesh Shah Charitable Pharmacy. We discussed our shared goal of reducing healthcare disparities and how a partnership could benefit not only their patients but the broader community. I wanted to ensure that the purpose behind the Ritesh Shah Charitable Pharmacy would endure long-term with the help of community partnerships. In fact, these organizations stood to benefit greatly, as their patients—those who qualify and live at or below 300% of the Federal Poverty Level (FPL)—would no longer need to seek medications elsewhere. In this way, we aimed to remove barriers to essential medications and create a sustainable cycle of health and well-being.

Collaborative Planning and Role Definition: Together, we mapped out how referrals, eligibility, and medication distribution would work. We clearly defined roles and responsibilities for each organization, ensuring smooth coordination and mutual accountability. This collaborative planning helped streamline processes, reduce duplication of efforts, and make it easier for patients to access timely care.

After many productive discussions with Parker Clinic, local FQHCs, and other community partners, we recognized the importance of creating forms and processes that would benefit both our organizations and, most importantly, our patients. Working together, we developed streamlined eligibility and referral forms to help patients access the Ritesh Shah Charitable Pharmacy's services without unnecessary hurdles. This collaboration allowed clinic staff to assist patients in completing paperwork and sending prescriptions directly, resulting in a seamless, supportive experience for those in need.

The next crucial step was building a comprehensive formulary of life-saving medications. We prioritized the most commonly prescribed and impactful medications in our community—those used to treat diabetes, heart disease, high blood pressure, and mental health conditions. Ultimately, our formulary included approximately 180–185 medications, primarily generics, to maximize reach and long-term sustainability. These choices weren't made lightly; they were informed by both clinical need in the community and my personal experience, especially the medications that were vital during my sister Rena's hospitalization.

By focusing on essential drugs like insulin, metformin, antihypertensives, statins, and key psychiatric medications, we aimed to close urgent gaps in care for uninsured and underserved patients. These are the very medications that often determine whether a patient remains stable or enters crisis, whether they retain hope or fall into despair. For example, we ensured the formulary included multiple types of insulin, critical oral diabetes agents, and medications for mental health, reflecting the complex and overlapping chronic conditions many patients face.

This careful selection process was rooted in a deep commitment to health equity. Our goal was to ensure that no patient would go without the medications that could prevent hospitalization, avoid complications, or even save their life. The formulary was designed not just to treat illness, but to provide patients—and their families—with the peace of mind that comes from consistent access to vital care.

Ultimately, these steps—developing shared forms, building a robust formulary, and centering on medications that matter most to our patients and to my own family—laid the foundation for the Ritesh Shah Charitable Pharmacy's mission. By working closely with Parker Clinic and our community partners, we built a model that actively addresses healthcare disparities and honors the legacy of those we serve, including my sister Rena.

Within just one year of opening the doors at the Ritesh Shah

Charitable Pharmacy, the "Pills to Purpose" journey proved stronger and more meaningful than ever. We had dispensed over $175,000 worth of life-saving medications, including $115,000 specifically for diabetes and insulin needs—$95,000 of that being insulin alone. Over 2,200 prescriptions were filled, and more than 240 underserved patients found hope and healing through our care. Today, 145 patients continue their maintenance therapies because we believed—because we cared.

These numbers aren't just statistics; they are stories. Lives touched. Prayers answered. They are the evidence of what happens when compassion leads the way, when purpose finds its home. Every pill counted. Every life mattered. With each prescription filled, we weren't just handing over medication; we were delivering dignity, health, and a future.

The mission that began from a place of love and loss grew stronger every single day, reminding us why we chose to serve and why we will never stop.

The Sacred Pause

That afternoon at the Ritesh Shah Charitable Pharmacy, the air was thick with the exhaustion and fulfillment that comes from a day spent serving others. As the last patients left, I gathered with Asha, our team, and our dedicated volunteers around the break table. The phone kept ringing-calls from Parker Clinic, Lunch Break, and local churches, each carrying messages of hope, gratitude, and urgent need. Word was spreading quickly: here was a place where no one would be turned away for lack of money, a sanctuary for the uninsured and the forgotten.

I looked around at the faces of my team, family by blood, all family by purpose. In that quiet, sacred moment, I turned to Asha, my partner in life and in this mission, and said, voice trembling, "You know, Asha, I went to India to mourn the loss of one life… and in return, God gave me a way to save hundreds." The room fell silent. Everyone felt the weight and beauty of that realization. It was never just about pills or prescriptions. It was about restoring dignity, hope, and health to those who had nowhere else to turn.

Asha's eyes filled with tears and pride as she smiled at me. "She's

smiling down on us, Ritesh. You found your purpose. We all did."
Around the table, volunteers nodded, some quietly wiping their eyes.
In that instant, we all knew-this wasn't just a pharmacy. It was a
temple of compassion, a beacon of hope, and Rena's light shining in
every life we touched. The mission we shared was bigger than any
one of us, and it was felt in every grateful patient, every story of a life
changed, every act of service.

A Family in Service

That evening, as the sun set over Red Bank, the sense of unity
in our small pharmacy was palpable. Our volunteers- drawn from
all walks of life-were bound together by a simple promise: to keep
serving, no matter how heavy the load. We knew that every call
for help, every prescription filled, was an act of love that could
ripple out into the world, multiplying hope in ways we could never
fully see.

The relationships we built with Parker Clinic, Lunch Break,
Pilgrim Baptist Church, and so many others became the backbone of
our mission. Together, we tackled health disparities, reaching those
most at risk and most often overlooked. The gratitude we received
was humbling, but the true reward was the sense of purpose that filled
our hearts. In those quiet moments after a long day, surrounded by
my team, I realized that grief had given way to something enduring.
Out of loss had come a legacy: a promise to serve, to heal, and to
honor Rena's memory by saving lives.

In that pharmacy, we were more than colleagues-we were a
family in service. And as we closed for the night, the vow was
unspoken but deeply understood: we would keep going, keep
giving, and keep shining Rena's light, one patient, one
prescription, one act of compassion at a time.

I'm proud to be part of a profession that makes a real difference
in people's lives! As a pharmacist, I've seen firsthand the impact we
have on our communities - from administering lifesaving vaccines
to helping patients manage chronic conditions. That's why almost 3
years ago I'm so thrilled to have started Ritesh Shah Charitable
Pharmacy to increase access for those who need it the most. By
providing free life-saving medications and immunizations to the
underserved, our operations and focus are on what really matters –

helping those who need it the most. Pharmacists provide compassionate, exceptional care to our patients each and every day, so let's celebrate the power of pharmacy and continue to make a positive impact together!

This letter and article from Ryan Nguyen, a Pharm.D. candidate at Rutgers Ernest Mario School of Pharmacy, was written as part of a preceptor newsletter requested by Dean Donna Feudo. In his reflection, Ryan describes his experience during the unprecedented uncertainty of the COVID-19 pandemic, when pharmacy students faced canceled or virtual rotations and widespread disruption.

Ryan details his APPE Community rotation at my independent pharmacy, DrugSmart Pharmacy, where I served as his preceptor. He highlights how I provided him with extensive learning opportunities, not only in pharmacy operations but also in the business side of pharmacy and the importance of community engagement. Ryan also notes the collaboration he experienced with my team at Legacy Pharmacy Group, which allowed him to gain insights into group purchasing and the broader pharmacy business landscape.

A significant part of Ryan's experience involved our rapid response to the pandemic. He participated in the rollout of no-cost COVID-19 nasopharyngeal swab testing across our pharmacies, working closely with our team to optimize the process. Ryan contributed by creating a patient-friendly pamphlet about COVID-19, which was distributed at all participating pharmacies to help educate patients in accessible language. This project allowed him to develop his communication skills and feel like an integral member of our healthcare team.

Ryan's letter expresses gratitude for the hands-on experience and mentorship he received, especially during such a challenging time. He credits this rotation with preparing him to become a compassionate and effective pharmacist, confident in his ability to help patients in the future.

Including this letter in my autobiography illustrates the impact of my mentorship and leadership on the next generation of pharmacists. It also highlights the importance of adaptability, collaboration, and community service during times of crisis. It's a testament to how our work at the pharmacy not only served patients but also helped shape future healthcare professionals.

The Language of Love Between My Asian Customer and Me

He often brought me Taiwanese green tea as a gift. I still have the sign he gave me hanging in my pharmacy in Holmdel.

In pharmacy, some of the most powerful moments come without a word being spoken.

Years ago, when I was still working at Bayshore Homecare Pharmacy in Holmdel, I met a patient I will never forget. He was an elderly Asian man who didn't speak any English. He had diabetes and epilepsy and came in frequently to refill his medications, mostly for his OneTouch Ultra test strips. But more than that, he came in just to see me. And somehow, even without words, we understood each other perfectly.

We communicated through simple hand gestures, nods, and something even deeper—eye contact. He would look at me, I'd look at him, and I just knew what he needed. It was as if he spoke through his heart. Sometimes he'd place his hands on the counter or gently roll up his sleeve, and I'd understand he wanted his blood sugar checked. And I always did—without hesitation.

I remember one day, as I was testing his sugar, I looked into his eyes and felt something I still can't fully describe. It was a mix of gratitude, trust, and something that felt like a blessing. It reminded me of caring for my own father. In that moment, I wasn't just helping a patient—I was serving someone's dad, someone's grandparent. And for me, that was more than enough.

At the time, I had Rutgers pharmacy students with me. They would observe these interactions and ask, "Why do you do that? We don't get paid for blood sugar testing." And they were right—there was no reimbursement, no billing code, no external reward. But I would smile and say, "This is what we do."

I couldn't fully articulate it then, but what I was trying to teach them was this: sometimes, purpose doesn't come with a price tag.

I wasn't doing it for money. I was doing it because it felt right. That man trusted me. He didn't have anyone else to help him. And in a world where patients are often just numbers or prescriptions, he reminded me why I became a pharmacist in the first place—to serve, to care, and to connect.

One day, he walked into the pharmacy with something wrapped carefully in brown paper. Inside was a framed piece of red calligraphy. He had written it—or had someone write it—for me. I couldn't read Chinese, but I knew it was something meaningful. Later, I had it translated. The message was deeply moving. It said that the kindness of a doctor or pharmacist is like the warmth of spring returning to the land, bringing life and healing to everything it touches. He called me and my staff "angels" who served patients with hearts. It was written in the spirit of Thanksgiving. From that moment on, my purpose became clearer. It wasn't just about filling prescriptions or managing numbers; it was about making a difference in someone's life.

That frame still hangs in my home. It's not just a decoration—it's a reminder. A reminder that love doesn't need language. That a pharmacist is not just someone behind a counter, but someone who can change a life with compassion. That even the smallest acts—like checking someone's sugar—can mean the world. Every time I look at it, I feel the pull of purpose.

This man didn't say a single word to me. But he taught me more about being a pharmacist than any classroom ever did. He showed me that healing comes from the heart, and that when we serve with love, we don't just fill prescriptions—we fulfill purpose.

Appendix

This book would not have been possible without the unwavering support and dedication of countless individuals. First and foremost, I extend my deepest gratitude to the patients of the charitable pharmacy. Your resilience, strength, and unwavering hope in the face of adversity inspired me every single day. Your stories are the heart of this narrative, and your contributions are truly immeasurable.

To the incredible team of volunteers, pharmacists, nurses, and support staff: your tireless commitment, compassion, and expertise formed the foundation of our success. You went above and beyond every single day, and I am deeply grateful for your contributions. A special thank you to Ayan Davis, whose organizational skills kept us all on track, and to Sarthak & Yash Shah, Dr. Murthy, and Dr. Patel, Dr Raval for their invaluable medical guidance.

I am also profoundly grateful to the numerous community organizations that partnered with us—your collaboration made so much possible. Special thanks to Susy Dyer and staff at Parker Clinic and, and the Lunch Break for providing initial partnership support. Your shared commitment to our community has been instrumental in everything we've achieved.

I am also thankful to each and every pharmacist for their dedication and commitment to their patients. This is not only my story but it's a story of all unsung pharmacists who have done so much for their patients. Community Pharmacists plays a key role everyday in helping patients so many unique ways.

Finally, I want to acknowledge the unwavering support of my family and friends, who stood by me through every challenge and celebrated every triumph. Your love, patience, and encouragement gave me the strength to keep going.

Author Biography

Ritesh Shah is a compassionate and experienced pharmacist with a strong entrepreneurial spirit and a deep dedication to community service. He brings a background in both pharmacy practice and non-fiction writing. Driven by a desire to address healthcare disparities, Ritesh founded and currently operates New Jersey's first and only charitable pharmacy—an endeavor that not only continues to serve those in need but also forms the foundation and inspiration for this book. His work underscores the power of community collaboration land the meaningful difference integrated care can make in the lives of vulnerable populations.

Beyond his work in pharmacy, Ritesh is a passionate advocate for health equity and continues to champion initiatives that promote access to quality healthcare for all. His journey is a testament to the ripple effect of heartfelt dedication and innovative solutions in the healthcare space.